CUTTHROAT CUPCAKES

A CURSED CANDY MYSTERY

CATE LAWLEY

ALSO BY CATE LAWLEY

VEGAN VAMP MYSTERIES

Adventures of a Vegan Vamp

The Client's Conundrum

The Elvis Enigma

The Nefarious Necklace

The Halloween Haunting

The Selection Shenanigans

The Cupid Caper

The Reluctant Renfield

NIGHT SHIFT WITCH MYSTERIES

Night Shift Witch

Star of the Party

Tickle the Dragon's Tail

Twinkles Takes a Holiday

DEATH RETIRED

Death Retires

A Date with Death

On the Street Where Death Lives

Wicked Bad Luck

For the most current listing of Cate's books, visit her website:

www.CateLawley.com

1
_____

I didn't profile my guests.

Not exactly.

But on days when I wasn't swamped with in-store shoppers and filling online orders, I practiced guessing the motivations of the people who entered my shop.

Every type of person came into Sticky Tricky Treats, my year-round, Halloween-themed candy store. Not an exaggeration, because everyone either *loved* sweets or *knew* someone who loved sweets.

And since I offered the best specialty, hand-crafted candies in town, I saw the sweet-tooth regulars, the special occasion shoppers, the apology gift buyers, and the seasonal crowd.

There'd been a lull the past hour, with online orders that didn't need to go out until tomorrow and only a customer or two in the store at a time. To pass the time, I played the "why candy, why today?" game while packing a few online orders.

There'd been the harried mother of three who just needed a little something special for herself on a tough day. The kids had been absent, likely in school, but the large purse and comfortable clothes hinted at busy mom, and the tired look in her eyes spoke volumes as to the type of day she'd been experiencing.

I placed a handful of lavender-lemon drops as an extra surprise for her inside her bag.

Then there was the PMSing thirty-something. She belonged to a subset of women I saw regularly in store: well aware that the sugar would give them a happy high for the moment but that they'd be suffering for the indulgence later.

I slipped a tiny packet of dark chocolate-covered almonds and hazelnuts into her bag. If she didn't like nuts or dark chocolate, so be it. But she'd probably feel slightly less terrible after eating them as a snack than she would after eating the milk chocolate caramels with sea salt. No judgment, though. I loved those salty-sweet candies during certain times of the month myself.

A few others passed through my shop, and I gave each of them my best effort. I was fairly confident in my guesses. Sussing out shoppers' motivations was one of my superpowers.

I looked at a customer, focused on what they needed, and poof, their candy motivation popped into my head. If they didn't come to my checkout counter with the treat I thought they needed, I slipped a little something extra into their bag. I could afford it. The shop had been on solid ground for about three years now. And it made me happy to give my guests a little something to make their day better.

Occasionally, a lone shopper whose candy motivation eluded me would cross my threshold.

Today was one of those rare instances.

I surreptitiously studied the man whose motivation would not be named. Still, nothing poofed into my head.

Tall, solidly built, scruffy-jawed with dirty-blond hair and a good sprinkling of gray in his short beard, there was nothing about him that should have prevented me from making a good guess.

It was possible I was distracted by his level-eight hotness, but I'd had the occasional nine come in the store and still managed to pinpoint their candy motivation.

He walked through my small shop examining each display. He paused in the sugar cupcake topper section, scrutinizing the pumpkin tops.

They weren't my favorite item. Once they were gone, I wasn't planning to make more. The idea had been for them to look like the sliced-off top of a pumpkin, like a pumpkin hat. The result wasn't entirely up to my standard, and I'd been in a bit of a mood when I'd been working on them. My ex had sent me a stream of less-than-friendly text messages that evening.

Not those poor pumpkin toppers' fault, but the product had been forever tainted in my mind.

Level Eight didn't pick up the pumpkin toppers. Rather, he continued his perusal of my wares, stopping only once more to give my candy sticks a thorough gander. Another non-favorite of mine, or at least the orangey-brown ones were. The evening I'd made them, I'd been peeved about some offensive behavior perpetrated upon my innocent lawn. My friend Betty, who happened to live a few houses away, had sent me video evidence of my least favorite neighbor blowing leaves into my yard...from across the street. Who did that?

Level Eight, with his unknown candy motivation, toured my entire stock of treats and happened to land on two of my least favorite candies, both made when I'd been less than my usual cheery self.

I didn't have a lot of foul moods. I was pretty upbeat in general, and especially in the last few years. Most days, I felt honored to be able to pursue my passion and live my dream, and that translated to a generalized sense of happiness, or at least contentment.

Not that I didn't have my moods and my bad days, but they were rare, so those two products truly were standout items.

And then, after walking through my entire shop and picking up not one item, he headed to the exit.

I was about to be offended—not many people entered Sticky Tricky Treats without purchasing at least one small goody—when he paused at the door and flipped the sign to closed.

"Excuse me!" The words flew from my mouth before I'd considered the danger factor.

A man had just isolated me in my own shop.

That could not be good.

I slid my hand casually to my rear jeans pocket, where I'd stashed my cell phone.

He paused, as if surprised by my objection. "The sugar pumpkins and the candy sticks are for sale?"

What? No, I put them out on the shelves with price tags for fun.

But I didn't voice my inappropriate thought. Instead, I replied calmly, "Yes. All of the candy on the shelves is for sale." Then again, I did give my customers little extras at no charge, so I added, "Though I do sometimes give samples."

Candy for sale and for sample, shocker, since this was a *candy shop*.

As evidenced by the sign on the door and all of the *candy*.

"Sophia Emmaline Dorchester, you are under arrest for the illegal sale and distribution of cursed candy and raw magic."

Oddly, it wasn't the "cursed" or the "magic" part of his impossible statement that first struck me.

Or even the arrested part.

It was the odd inflection in Level Eight's speech. I thought he might possibly be German, though his English was practically native.

Then I realized some strange (possibly German) man was attempting to arrest me.

And *then* I realized he'd accused me of selling "cursed" candy and raw "magic."

Clearly, this man was having a break with reality inside my candy store.

Oh. My. God.

He just flipped the lock on my shop door.

2

I was going to die.

Murdered in my favorite place in the whole world, surrounded by my lovingly crafted candies (with the exception of the pumpkin toppers and the candy sticks, naturally).

Thirty-seven years old, never married, and no kids. I'd never even been to Canada! I'd lived in Idaho for five years, and I'd never been to Canada.

But that was all moot, because a deranged man had stormed my shop, and he was going to murder me dead. I wouldn't be around anymore, and I definitely wouldn't be going to Canada.

I eyed the potentially murderous man. Interestingly, he didn't *look* deranged.

He headed toward me, but his path veered and he landed once again in front of the candy sticks. He removed a pair of gloves from a pocket. Black, like the ones my colorist used when she bleached and dyed my hair.

Then, gloved up, he gathered my orange and brown striped candy sticks and deposited them on the counter in front of me.

Next he retrieved the pumpkin cupcake toppers and placed them next to the candy sticks.

"A bag?" he asked. As if he were shopping.

Except he wasn't shopping. He'd just "arrested" me, and I suspected this was his version of evidence collection.

When I failed to comply, he leaned over the counter and grabbed one himself.

As he leaned forward, I leaned back. He might not be waving a weapon, but he was behaving in a highly suspect manner.

He stuffed the offending candy into the purloined bag. "Do you have an employee you can call to cover for you?"

Implying I would be leaving? With him? Um, no. But his comment reminded me of my cell. The phone currently tucked in my back pocket.

What was going on with my sense of self-preservation? A guy busts into my shop and locks us inside together, for all I know with plans to murder me dead, and I didn't even pick up my phone to dial 9-1-1?

If I could whack my intuition, I would. It was clearly on the fritz.

I ignored his question and indicated the candy stick display. "I think you missed a few of the orange and brown ones."

The plan had been to snag my phone from my back pocket when he looked away. Except he didn't look at the display. His gaze remained firmly glued on me.

"I got them all." Level Eight crossed his arms. "Your phone won't work."

My hand had slipped to my back pocket without me even realizing it, giving away my intentions.

This guy. He probably thought he'd put a spell on my phone, and hocus-pocus, abracadabra, he was going to prevent me from calling.

But if he *thought* that was true, then maybe I could sneak a call before he realized his "magic" wasn't working. I retrieved it and dialed 9-1-1.

Or I tried to.

A solid black screen greeted me.

The delusional man had not abracadabra'd my phone dead. He hadn't. I must have forgotten to charge it last night.

I inched closer to the phone next to the register. Yes, my store had a landline. And as much as I begrudged that bill each month, right now I was doing a little dance over the fact that I had another way to reach out for help.

Level Eight arched his eyebrows. "Go ahead. Try it."

Dead. Just like I was going to be, because I was trapped with a murdery magic man.

Okay, I didn't really think that. But I was trapped in my shop with a guy who planned really well and definitely had his own weird agenda. Taking out both of my phones would have required a lot of planning.

Ugh. I'd almost prefer a murdery magic man to someone who plotted my takedown with such meticulous care.

"I'm confused. I should call someone to cover for me, but not really because my cell is dead and you've cut my landline somehow."

He retrieved a cell from his cargo pants. Yeah, he'd woken up this morning and had a moment when he looked in his closet and thought that cargo pants were a good choice.

And yet, I'd still found him attractive when he'd walked through my door. Maybe he was an eight-point-five-level hotness, since I'd initially looked right past those tragic pants.

He lifted the phone. "You have someone you can call?"

A stranger who claimed to believe in magic and

to have the ability to arrest me was confiscating (stealing, because where was the cash?) my candy and illegally detaining me, but now he wanted me to take his phone and call an available employee—which I did not have—so that my store could remain open. He was a considerate delusional person?

"Uh..." I was having a hard time fitting everything that was happening right now into my brain and making it come together in a way that made sense.

"An employee?" He prompted once more as he jiggled the phone in his hand.

"I've only got one part-timer, and she's got midterms right now."

He shrugged, as if that was just fine with him. It probably was, since he could murder-kidnap-arrest me even more easily without an employee wondering why they'd been called in last minute. "You'll have to close the shop, then."

Since he'd already done that when he flipped my sign to CLOSED and locked the door, what was I supposed to say?

Except I was feeling contrary, so I said, "No."

Because...no.

I would not be complicit in my own kidnapping. And since this whacko had yet to pull some kind of weapon out of one of those many pockets of his, I was calling his bluff. Also, I wasn't feeling nearly as threatened by this man as the situation called for, and that was making me brave.

He frowned, as if my behavior confused him.

My behavior confused *him*.

Me, the lucid person who refused to believe in curses and raw magic or to be complicit in her own fake arrest.

Except, I wasn't entirely with it, because I'd accidentally refused the use of his phone, which I could have used to call for help.

Self-preservation fail. Intuition fritzing. Clearly, I wasn't made for handling emergencies.

I'd smack my head, but at this rate, I wasn't entirely sure I wouldn't give myself a concussion. That was just the kind of day this was turning into.

"Before we leave, I need to see your logbook." When I stared at him in confusion—because, what logbook?—he said, "Your logbook? Where you record the names and contact information for the recipients of magical items."

'Kay. First, I was skipping the issue of "magical items." I don't curse candy, I don't distribute raw magic, and I don't sell magical items. Just because my candy store was Halloween-themed, that didn't mean I believed in ghosts, witches, and warlocks. Nor did I dabble in spells, jinxes, or hexes.

But this guy apparently believed in *all* the

magical things, and I wasn't about to tip his world view off its axis right now—if I even could.

As for the logbook?

"You're kidding me, right?" I flashed him an incredulous scowl. "We're not selling guns in here, mister."

"Bastian."

"Sorry?"

"Bastian Heissman, regional representative for the International Criminal Witch Police." He pulled a wallet from yet another pocket. How many pockets did those terrible pants have?

His wallet contained a shiny badge that he was now displaying with a great deal of confidence.

Did delusional people have props?

This was news to me. I'd never been cornered and locked in my shop by a lunatic intent on arresting me for made-up charges. Then again, he had done enough prep to take out my cell and landline, so fake credentials fit in nicely with his careful planning.

"I want to see your badge." I mostly asked to mess with him just a little bit.

He handed it over without hesitation. Freakishly, it looked and felt real. Solid. I'd expected something like a child's Wild West tin badge, I guess. It even had *International Criminal Witch Police* stamped on it.

And since I had possession of his wallet, I flipped through it. I'd been right about his slight accent. He had a German identity card, as well as an Idaho driver's license. There were also a few credit cards. Each card had his name, Bastian Heissman, printed on it.

I returned it and then held out my hand palm up. "Your phone."

"No."

"Worth a try." I leaned on the counter. "You know you're going to jail."

"Prison. Jail is a temporary holding facility where convicted criminals sentenced to a term less than one year serve their time."

He sounded a little like a cop. Or a guy who knew cop-like stuff.

"So you're saying you recognize what you're doing is illegal and that it's serious enough to warrant a longer sentence."

He sighed. "I don't have time for this. As you know, the International Witch and Warlock Code of Conduct outlines—"

"No, Bastian. No, I do *not* know, because I've never heard of the international code of whatever."

Honesty seemed like the best policy. I wasn't denying the existence of magic, only the knowledge of some fictional rule book with fake rules that Bastian seemed to think I'd violated.

My response didn't elicit a sigh this time. Rather

than annoyed, frustrated, and generally impatient, now he looked concerned. "Who was your mentor?"

"Uh, Cat helped me set up my books. Betty, my super cool elderly neighbor, she helps with taste-testing. Oh, and Brian." I wrinkled my nose, because even saying his name made me want to scream or eat a lot of milk chocolate caramel with sea salt. "My ex, Brian, helped with—"

"No, your witch mentor."

And here it was. What I'd been trying to avoid. "No witch mentor, Bastian, because I'm not a witch. Because witches aren't actually real." I waved at the Halloween décor in my shop—witches, ghosts, and vampires, inclusive—and said, "Not real. Any of it."

A determined light sparked in his eyes, and then he whipped out a pair of handcuffs from one of his gazillion pockets. Yet another reason to hate those pants.

Wait—handcuffs? No. No-no.

Except, yes. Bastian Heissman, regional rep of some imaginary witch squad, was snapping hand-cuffs on me. Had already cuffed me, in fact. How had that happened so fast?

"You can't arrest me for...for...whatever you're arresting me for!"

I couldn't have an arrest record. I was no crimi-nal. Ack! Now I was buying into his delusion. That was wrong. So wrong. I would not be brainwashed.

The fear that had been trickling away ever since its initial spike with the locking of my front door now flared. "You're definitely going to murder-kidnap me, aren't you?"

The counter still separated us, which was a testament to Bastian's cuffing skills. I couldn't recall exactly how the restraints had gone from his hands to around my wrists.

He ignored my question. Worse, he ignored me. He pulled out his cell and made a phone call. "I need transport."

"I'm not getting in your murder van." Pretty sure I screeched that loud enough that whoever was on the other end of the line could hear it.

"Yeah. Give me a five-second delay." Bastian tucked away his phone in one of his various pockets, grabbed his bag of purloined candy with one hand, and then leaned further across the counter to grab my upper arm with the other.

Then everything went black.

3

W as that—I inhaled—coffee?

And not the over-roasted, burnt variety. The aroma surrounded me. I inhaled again, because I loved the smell of coffee. It was next only to the smell of baking bread in my inventory of favorite food scents.

And yes, I was a confectioner who loved the smell of baked bread above candy and other sweets. I possessed a number of odd quirks, and that particular preference didn't come near to topping the list.

"I think she's awake." The voice sounded worried. And male. And young.

"She's definitely awake." This came from a woman. Also, young but much less worried.

"Sophia." *That* voice I recognized. My abductor, Bastian Heissman.

I groaned. No one called me Sophia except my great-aunt, and that was only because I was named after her. I suspected her persistence indicated an inflated ego more than a failing memory. Then again, she did claim her memory wasn't exactly the best.

"Well, looks like you might have maimed this one," the woman said.

"No way," the young man replied. "I'm careful. I'm always careful."

Huh. I didn't *feel* maimed. I felt...okay. Probably.

Pretty sure I was reclining on a sofa, and opening my eyes seemed like *a lot* of effort, but otherwise no obvious complaints.

On the plus side, I wasn't cuffed. I was fairly sure I'd been cuffed earlier.

Cuffed or not, maimed or not, I couldn't hang out all evening listening to people I didn't know talk about me. With a concerted effort, I willed my eyes open to find that I was, as I'd predicted, lying on a sofa.

Since the view of the ceiling didn't reveal much, I moved to sit up.

Bad choice. Very bad.

My head exploded with pain before I got a look at the worried guy or the flippant woman.

Bastian loomed over me and put his hand on my shoulder. "Take it easy."

As if he needed to hold me there or tell me not to move. Please. I wasn't going anywhere in a hurry. I disliked pain intensely.

The woman sniggered. "Told you. Maimed."

"I'm not maimed," I whispered. "But I do feel like a bag of jawbreakers knocked me on the head."

"That's weirdly specific," the woman said.

"Not really. I'm a candy maker, and I've had a bag of jawbreakers dropped on my head." I slowly shifted toward the group but couldn't help a small moan.

"I can fix that for you, if you like," the woman said.

Both Bastian and the worried young man said, "No!" before I had the chance to say, "Yes," and ask how quickly.

"I'll fix it," Bastian said.

"Uh, I think you dropped the jawbreakers."

He looked confused, or maybe as if he was translating in his head—odd, because his English was exceptional—and then he said, "I didn't hit you. Not with a bag of jawbreakers or anything else. You didn't handle the transport very well."

Transport...

Wait a second. I'd been in my shop, Bastian had phoned someone requesting transport, and then he'd grabbed my arm.

That was all I could remember.

"Did you drug me?"

The woman—a short, curvy, twenty-something with dark brown, almost black hair and a perfectly executed bold red lip—said, "No, he didn't drug you. That's not Bastian's style. Poisons and potions seem like they'd be more up *your* alley, what with your propensity for cursing edibles."

"Seriously? With the cursed candy garbage again? How many times do I have to say it? I didn't curse my candy."

"Yeah, except you did." The brunette rolled her eyes. "You made the candy. And the candy is cursed. Ergo, you cursed the candy."

"What's your name?" I really wanted a name to put with that obnoxious attitude and red lipstick.

"Here we go," the worrier muttered. He was average height, dark-headed and with just enough facial hair to be interesting. His age was difficult to determine, because even with the scruff, he had a youthful look.

The brunette glared. At him, at me. At the world in general. "Sabrina."

If I was reading this situation correctly, the three people locked in this aromatic room with me right now believed they were witches. The whole International Criminal Witch Police schtick pointed to that conclusion.

And now I was chit-chatting with Sabrina...the witch.

I swallowed a laugh, because one, inappropriate, and two, laughter was guaranteed to make my head explode.

Sabrina, with her dark hair, bright red lipstick, and plunging cleavage looked nothing like the wholesome blond from the TV show of my childhood, and yet, I couldn't help but pair the two.

"Not a single word. Don't say it. Don't—"

But I couldn't help myself. "Sabrina the teenage witch." I pressed my lips together, because laughter equaled pain. Also, I doubted that any verbal expression of humor would be tolerated by Sabrina the not-teenage witch.

Shame on me for pushing her buttons. I really shouldn't antagonize her. We short ladies needed to stick together. Also, she seemed like she might be a terrible friend but an even worse enemy.

"You done?" she asked.

I started to nod then thought better of it given the pain that was waiting to explode in my head and said, "I think so. Sorry. It was a compulsion."

"Yeah, ever since that remake came out—" She squinted at the look on my face. "The new one? Has a horror vibe?"

I hadn't a clue what she was talking about.

She rolled her eyes. "Never mind."

"Can I fix you now?" Bastian asked.

"If you can make the second worst headache I've ever experienced disappear, then yes, please fix me."

Bastian knelt next to me, and I got a whiff of him. He smelled like cardamom and ginger and cinnamon and a touch of citrus and—

"Sophia?" he asked with more than a hint of annoyance in his tone.

"Huh? My name's Lina. I don't go by Sophia." And I would not sniff him. Even if he did smell like the yummiest man I'd ever smelled. He'd gone from level eight and a half to eleven. How was I supposed to think around an eleven? There wasn't even such a thing as an eleven.

"Right. *Lina*, can I start?" His hand was inches from my head.

"Sure. Yeah. Do your thing." Maybe he'd magic finger massage my pain away. Wait, that sounded weird.

He placed three fingers on my temple.

There was no sparkle, no lights, no rhyming words, but the man performed magic.

A warmth spread from his fingers. It wasn't a warmth of increased temperature. It was more a feeling of goodwill. A sense of coziness.

He did that—with his touch.

And my headache? Gone.

"K, so this magic you guys are all convinced

exists? I'm totally on board." As Bastian's hand dropped away, I sat up, completely pain free. "I'm a believer. Call me a convert. How did you do that?"

"Aw, man. Seriously, Bastian? You do a little healing woo-woo, and she's all, *yeah, magic is real.*" The worried guy was looking a lot less worried now. He looked peeved. "I ship her body from downtown Boise to the Bench, but that's nothing."

Ship my body? What?

Bastian was still kneeling next to me, and I got a good look at his dreamy blue eyes. Oh. My. God. I didn't just call his eyes dreamy. That wasn't okay, even in my head. I blamed his supercharged, spice-scented pheromones.

"Miles, you're freaking her out." Sabrina examined me. "Or Bastian's freaking her out." She gave me a knowing look, and her lips quirked into a half smile. "Definitely Bastian."

"Where am I?" That seemed the safest question to ask. It had absolutely nothing to do with healing magic or delicious smells.

A quick scan of the room revealed we were in an office.

There was an exterior and interior door, an extremely tidy desk with a sleek laptop and little else on it. Behind the desk was a bookshelf with a bunch of journals. The kind that had metal clasps and a lock, except they weren't pink and purple with glitter and intended for the twelve-year-old girl, secret diary crowd. These were made of old leather in an array of dark colors.

Who locked their journals besides preteen girls with nosy older brothers?

"Magic Beans," Bastian said. Out of the blue, as if a reference to Jack and the Beanstalk meant something to me.

"You asked where we are." Bastian was looking grumpier by the minute. "We're in my coffee shop, Magic Beans."

Oh. Okay, that made way more sense than a random story reference. Except... "What witch calls their coffee shop Magic Beans? And I thought you were a cop."

"Not a witch, a person with a sense of humor, and I am."

It took me a second to parse Sebastian's response, until I figured out that he'd answered my three questions in the order I'd, implicitly, asked them.

He claimed he had a sense of humor, but did he really? I hadn't seen evidence of it.

"So, the International Criminal Witch Police is run by a bunch of people who aren't witches."

Sabrina lifted a hand. "Witch, but I'm just his peon." She glared at Bastian.

"And head barista," the peon's boss added.

Worried guy, aka Miles, lifted a hand. "Warlock, transport expert, research guru, tech advisor, and also proud to be a barista in the best coffee shop you've never heard of." Then he pointed to Bastian. "Wizard."

"What's the difference?" I asked. "Between witches and warlocks and wizards?"

"What rock have you been hiding under?" Sabrina asked.

Hoping it was rhetorical, I didn't answer.

"No, seriously," Sabrina said. "How do you not know, like, anything?"

That was just offensive. "I know how to make candy. Really good candy."

Miles nodded. "True fact. Your toffee is amazing. Oh, and also those mint chocolate things with the candy shell?"

"Holland mints." Those were quite tasty. Naturally, mine were orange, green, and purple, rather than the more traditional pastel colors.

"Yes, Holland mints. They're so good." He realized that Bastian and Sabrina were giving him the eye, and he blushed. "I've never actually been *inside* the store. I didn't know that she was selling cursed candy."

"That's true, he hasn't. Well, not when I've been manning the counter, anyway. And, I'm not selling cursed candy."

Sabrina looked at me, cocked her head, and then grinned broadly. That couldn't be good. Her grin widened when she saw the look on my face. "You do know you're a witch, right?"

I coughed as I failed to entirely swallow the laugh that burbled in my very nonmagical chest. "Uh, no."

"Yes," Bastian replied. He studied me then said, "I need you to agree to a lie detector spell."

"What? Why?" A magical lie-detecting test sounded ominous. Intrusive, for sure. Also, shouldn't I have an attorney if things were getting that real?

Sabrina made an incredulous sound. "Because it's really hard to believe that you really don't know you're a witch. You're kinda old for that."

"Basically," Bastian agreed, but then shook his head. "Not the age part, the fact that you're unaware of your magic. Your ignorance would change everything."

"It's not a big deal," Miles chimed in, "so long as you don't plan to lie."

Maybe I should have dithered, asked for more information, heck, even asked for the questions first. But this was the guy who'd cured my headache. Despite having locked us in my store earlier and disabling my phones, he seemed a stand-up sort of guy. Maybe he wasn't warm and fuzzy, but...I trusted him. And that's saying a lot given the fact he arrested me.

"All right." I bit my lip. "What do I have to do?"

I accepted a rock Bastian retrieved from his desk. Actually, not a rock. It was a translucent blue-green crystal roughly the length of my hand and the circumference of perhaps a quarter.

"You understand that as long as you hold the crystal, I'll hear every lie you tell." Bastian waited for my agreement, then asked, "Did you know you were a witch before today?"

Easy enough. "No."

"Are you aware of any witches in your family?"

I gave him a funny look. "Can I just say that I didn't believe witches existed before today?"

He arched an eyebrow. "Is that what you're saying?"

"I didn't believe in witches before today. Not the kind with magic. Not in my family or elsewhere."

He paused before asking his next question, but when it came it surprised me. Actually, no, it made me angry. "Did you intentionally poison your candy sticks?"

"No!"

"Or your cupcake toppers?"

In a much calmer voice, I said, "No."

He held his hand out. "The crystal?" he prompted, when I didn't return it.

"Oh." I handed it over quickly. "Uh, then that's all?"

"Not exactly." He stowed the pretty blue-green crystal in his desk drawer again. "But it's enough to keep the cuffs off you for now."

It seemed I was still under arrest. That wasn't great.

"You asked about witches and warlocks," Bastian said. When I gave him a confused look, he said, "Earlier. You asked what the difference was. Witches and warlocks are one and the same. It's considered somewhat outdated to differentiate by gender."

"Which is why y'all are the International Criminal Witch Police and not the International Criminal Witch and Warlock Police?" I asked.

"I think it's because ICWP is shorter." Miles shrugged. "Occasionally, we're practical."

Instantaneous transport, crystals that could spot lies, speedy cures for headaches—practical was one word for them and their magic.

"And wizards?" I asked Bastian, since he was one. "What are wizards?"

"Not witches."

I swallowed my groan of annoyance. He knew I was at an uncomfortable disadvantage. That I was coming from a place of complete ignorance. He had magical proof via a lie-detecting crystal of that very fact.

I waited for an answer, but awkward silence didn't elicit further explanation. For all I knew, the difference between wizards and witches was some weird cultural taboo, so I shifted to another glaringly obvious question. "I still don't understand how I got here."

Miles's eyes lit up. "Oh, I'll take that one. I am the transport expert. So, it's all about the pull, not the push."

"This again." Sabrina rolled her eyes. "I'm getting coffee."

Not that she was soliciting orders, but I had woken in a strange place surrounded by the magical equivalent of law enforcement... "I'll take an espresso. One shot with a dollop of cream."

She was out the door in a flash, not bothering to ask if Bastian or Miles needed anything.

And she was Magic Beans's head barista. Maybe there was a reason I'd never heard of it.

Bastian seated himself behind the desk—most likely *his* desk, since this was his coffee shop—while Miles rubbed his hands together.

"So, transport," Miles said as he dropped into an armchair.

"Right" I said. "Pushing and pulling."

"Wrong." Miles frowned like I'd disappointed him. "No pushing. Only pulling. A transport expert,

like myself, can pull another individual through
space—"

"But not time," Bastian clarified.

"No! Not time." Miles looked appalled at the very
prospect. "No. That would be bad. Very bad."

Bastian's eyes glinted with something that might
possibly be...humor?

I shot an amused glance his way. "Shame on you.
Don't tease the transport expert."

Then I turned all of my attention to Miles's
explanation. Well, ninety-nine percent of my attention. I couldn't completely ignore Bastian, much as I
might like to.

"I know where I am," Miles said, "and I can tag
other people in advance. So then I can pull them to
the known location—my location—as long as
they've been tagged."

"Wait, are we talking about 'beam me up, Scotty'
transportation?" My lack of any memory of how I
arrived at Magic Beans, blacking out, my massive
headache, it all added up to... "I wasn't drugged. You
beamed me here?"

Miles's cute, scruffy face took on a perturbed
cast. "I mean, I like to call it shipping or transporting
and not beaming, because we're not living in an
episode of *Star Trek*, but sure." He crossed his arms
and eyeballed me. "Are you freaking out?"

Was I freaking out? "I think I'm freaking out

about not freaking out." Because I'd been blasted into oblivion, my parts potentially floating in the ether to be magically reconstituted by a guy who looked like he was barely out of college.

Bastian made a grumpy noise. "English isn't my first language, but I don't usually have such difficulty understanding Idahoans."

"I'm from Texas." He seemed to accept that as adequate explanation, but I was fairly certain he'd missed my point. "What I was trying to say is that I don't understand how I can possibly believe that I was magically beamed from my shop to here."

"But you do." Bastian made it sound like there was no question. As if it was a matter of course that I'd accept my magical beaming—transport—across Boise.

"It's because you're a witch," Miles explained. "Oh, coffee!"

Sabrina walked in bearing a tray with four drinks. I wasn't sure how she'd managed to open the door without dropping the whole thing. Probably magic, because why not? I'd bought into the mass delusion, so might as well embrace it. But it was also quite possible that, as a barista, she possessed solid tray-wielding skills.

"Thanks," Miles said as he accepted a small cup. He took a sip and sighed in blissful appreciation.

"Like I was saying, you're a witch. You're genetically preprogrammed to believe in magic."

"I call bull crap on that." I murmured my thanks for the demitasse she handed me. It smelled fantastic. "My cousins were convinced their house was haunted when we were growing up. I never believed that. Oh, and my great-aunt— not the one I'm named after, a different one—she used to claim she could see the future. Also didn't buy that."

"Because that's not magic." Bastian accepted his coffee from Sabrina without a word. No thanks, no smile, no acknowledgment. "You're more likely to recognize and accept real magic."

I glared at him, but he didn't get the hint.

Sabrina winked at me. "It's okay. He pays; that's enough."

And she'd given him a pink mug with a delicate handle and small glittering hearts scattered across its surface. Score one for Sabrina.

He looked between the two of us, again as if he were translating in his head.

I drank my exceptional espresso with exactly the right amount of cream and tried to keep my annoyance at recent events to a minimum. Nothing like a rotten mood to ruin good caffeine.

Miles was blissfully and obliviously enjoying his brew. Sabrina was alternating between watching me and Bastion. She looked way too amused for my liking.

And Bastian? He leaned back in his chair as if he had nothing better to do than accuse me of cursing candy, slapping some cuffs on me, and shipping my unconscious self halfway across Boise.

"Why am I here?" I asked.

Miles lost his blissful look. "Oh, boss. Don't tell me you forgot to officially arrest her before you had me ship her here."

"No. He arrested me. For the distribution and sale of cursed candies, I believe. But it's garbage. I didn't do it." And even if I did, a cop wouldn't zap me to his wizardly lair, remove my cuffs, and ply me with coffee unless he wanted something from me. "And now you know I didn't do it."

Sabrina sighed. "I'm telling you, Lina. You did it. You made the candies, the candies are cursed, ergo—"

"I cursed the candies. Whatever. You know what I mean. If I did it, it wasn't on purpose, because I didn't know about magic. The lie detector confirmed it, so why am I here?" I pinned Bastian with a stare.

He set his pink coffee cup down. "I'm offering you a deal."

I was sticking to my story: innocent until proven guilty and all that...assuming the witch justice system worked like the non-witch version.

That was an uncomfortable thought.

And it went downhill from there.

Working on the hypothesis that I was actually a witch and possessed magic, what if those particularly foul moods I'd been in when creating my alleged cursed candies had *actually* cursed the candy?

What if someone had become ill—or worse—from eating my candy?

Finally, I spoke into the silence. "What kind of deal?"

"You help me find the person who used your cursed cupcake topper to kill a man, and I won't charge you as an accessory to murder."

4

M urder?" Pretty sure that was me speaking, but it was a little echoey sounding. I carefully placed the demitasse on the small coffee table next to the sofa. "What? How?"

"She doesn't look so good." The hint of worry was back in Miles's voice again.

"Boss, did you not mention someone used the raw magic in her supercharged cursed cupcake topper to off someone?" Sabrina still wasn't sounding too worried and possibly was having a good time pointing out a potential failing on the part of her employer.

My cupcake topper had *killed* someone. "How do you kill a person with a cupcake topper?"

"When it's drenched with as much raw magic as yours are, so many different ways." Sabrina ticked off options on her fingers. "As a potion additive, as part of a ritual, ingested by the magic-user to add to their own power. Yeah, those are probably the top three."

"Yours was used to create a potion which was then added to a beverage the victim drank, from what we can tell," Miles added helpfully.

I really didn't feel so good. Good thing I was still sitting on the sofa. Except, that might not be enough. I lowered my head between my knees.

After a few seconds, the room stopped spinning.

A few more seconds and I felt like I could lift my head without negative repercussions.

All three occupants of the room were eyeing me with some trepidation.

"I'm not going to throw up." I was *pretty sure* I wasn't. And if it came to that, I'd certainly make an effort to hit the trash can. Which led to a scan of the room. The only reasonable receptacle was the wastepaper basket under Bastian's desk.

"Don't ralph on the rug." Sabrina's dry tone was accompanied by a glare. "I found it, since Bastian hates to shop, and I like it."

It covered most of the empty space in the middle of the office. And it was a combination of various shades of aqua, teal, and blue—much like my hair.

It was pretty. Soothing. An interesting choice given that Sabrina was whatever the opposite of soothing was. Turbulent? Contrary? Rude?

Bastian interrupted my musings. "What do you think of the offer?"

I wasn't reeling or about to lose the contents of my stomach, but I also didn't appreciate being confronted with the reality of my predicament quite so quickly.

"Give a girl a minute, why don't you?" I snapped.

To breathe.

To think.

To decide if I could work closely with a level-eleven hottie who smelled like Christmas and cuddles.

What? Where did that come from?

Christmas?

And cuddles?

Cuddles didn't even have a smell. I was losing it. All this magic nonsense, my first run-in with the law, being magically "shipped" halfway across town, it had all scrambled my brain.

I needed to slow this train down. "I'm not sure I understand my options fully."

"You don't want to be charged as an accessory to murder," Miles said with a look of utter confusion on his face. "You really don't."

"No, I don't." I didn't even need to know what the sentence for such a crime was. I knew I didn't want to face those charges. "How do you even know that it was *my* magic in the potion that killed this person?"

Bastian sighed. And if I didn't know better, I'd think he was exasperated. "We have tests, not that we needed them in this instance. I knew as soon as I walked into your shop and spotted your cupcake toppers. The orange and brown candy sticks were a bonus. We'll be destroying those for you. You're welcome."

I blinked. I wasn't thanking him. Maybe I should, because how did one dispose of raw cursing magic? But I wasn't about to thank the man who'd arrested me and was now twisting my arm to make a deal with me.

"We got a hot tip about a secret raw magic supplier operating out of your candy shop." Miles spoke those words as if they weren't completely insane. As if he hadn't equated me to an arms dealer.

Arms dealing and hot tips aside, one result this ridiculous conversation was having was that I was beginning to fully, truly, viscerally grasp that witches weren't just a Halloween fashion statement.

I was beginning to actually believe that... "I'm a witch."

"That's an excellent place to start." Bastian gestured to himself, Miles, and Sabrina. "And we're the regional law enforcement branch of the International Criminal Witch Police."

I eyed Bastian, whom I'd pegged as a few years

older than me, possibly in his early forties, then his "support staff."

Miles and Sabrina looked like they were barely out of college.

"The three of you are it? For the entire city of Boise?"

Bastian huffed. "City? Town."

"Hey, now. No smack-talking Boise." I'd only lived here five years, but that was long enough to recognize that the place definitely had its charms.

"I'm not talking smack. I'm stating a fact. It's a town, not a city. But to answer your question, the three of us cover the greater Boise area." His lips pulled into a grimace. "Insomuch as there is a greater metro area."

I let that comment slide. Better to pick my battles sensibly, and fighting over the German import's bias against Boise wasn't looking like a winner.

"What are the specifics of this deal you're offering me?" I prompted.

Bastian's eyes were at half mast, and he leaned back in his chair. If I didn't know better, I'd say he could care less about the outcome of this negotiation. And this was a negotiation.

They had proof that a candy from my shop had been used to murder someone. Whether I'd imbued that cupcake topper with cursing magic or not—and

I couldn't see who else *could* have—I'd certainly sold it.

It seemed as if Bastian and his band of magical coppers had all the power, but I knew better. Something told me that he wanted my help. Badly.

It was like the candy motivations of Sticky Tricky Treats patrons; I simply *knew* that my answer mattered to him.

"As I said, you help me catch the murderer, and I don't charge you as an accessory. You provided the means by which the victim was killed. I have ample grounds to charge you."

He waved his police authority in my face purely to unsettle me; I was sure.

I would not be unsettled. Well, I would, but I wouldn't let him know it. "And the duration of this agreement?"

"However long it takes to catch the killer."

The question had surprised him, except why? A contract with no defined completion time? Um, no. Did I look like an idiot?

"You've got a week of my time, after shop hours. After that, killer or no killer, you cut me loose."

He huffed out an exasperated breath. "No."

That was it. No counteroffer. He really didn't get this negotiation thing.

"Why do you even want to work with me?"

"It was our idea," Sabrina said, surprising the heck out of me. "Mine and Miles's."

"We think you're harmless, but he's a stickler for the rules." Miles jerked his head in Bastian's direction. "Who openly sells raw cursing magic right out of their retail shop? We didn't know that you were an undiscovered witch. We were thinking more along the lines of an inventory flub or your assistant putting out the wrong stock, since she's one hundred percent magicless."

The boss man was not happy that Miles had shared his opinion of my harmlessness. But I was. Totally harmless. Completely.

"It's not like just having cursing magic lying around is illegal." Miles slouched in his armchair and kicked his legs out in front of him. As if talking about magic and curses was no big deal.

"Exactly," Sabrina agreed. "It's what you do with it that will get you in trouble."

Miles said, "Selling it is definitely bad."

As if I hadn't figured that part out already.

"We thought you could help, so long as you weren't weaponizing your wares on purpose and trying to start a not-so-secret, not-so-underground supply ring for magical criminals in Boise." Sabrina shrugged, as if the idea of me as a criminal mastermind (especially a bad one) wasn't the most absurd proposition to have ever been uttered. "Besides, who hasn't played around a little with some minor cursing?"

"Me," I replied. "I haven't played around with minor cursing. Or major cursing. Or any kind of cursing."

"Well, that's just not true." Sabrina smiled at me. She even looked like she meant it, in an "I'm maybe a little impressed with your accidental skills" way. Which she proved with her next comment. "You created the raw material for what became a murder weapon, and it wasn't even on purpose."

The implication being that if I really put my mind to it, I could make something even more dastardly?

"Thanks for that." I smiled back, baring my teeth. "Yay for me."

"No, jail for you," Bastian said, finally breaking his lengthy silence.

And he claimed he had a sense of humor.

"My offer?" I reminded him. "One week, after shop hours, my undivided attention."

He didn't flinch...and yet, I could feel it. He wanted my help.

Expression blank, he said, "You have two choices. You can go back to your shop and pretend like none of this has happened."

That sounded fabulous, and also like I might be missing the punchline.

Bastian continued, "In which case, you could be charged as an accessory to the murder of Bartholomew Bitters."

Why did he have to tell me the name of the victim? Poor old Bartholomew Bitters. He had to be old, right? With a name like that... Except I didn't need to be worried about Mr. Bitters. I needed to be worried about me.

"Could be?" I jumped on the specific wording of Bastian's statement. "You said I *could be* charged."

"Technically, I should charge you," Bastian said. "Ignorance of the law is no defense. And if you don't give me something, some demonstration of mitigation and cooperation, then I still may have to."

I *hated* being strong-armed. Stubborn to the last, I asked, "What happens to someone convicted as an accessory to murder? I don't suppose it's a fine, is it?"

"The Witch Tribunal isn't fond of fines," Bastian said.

Of course they're not. They were a witch tribunal. They probably went for stoning and hanging.

Bastian's lips twitched. "Don't worry. They got rid of the death penalty years ago."

More sniggering from Sabrina. "Like *three* years ago."

I must have looked as freaked-out as I felt,

because Bastian glared at Sabrina. "Sabrina's kidding, Lina."

"Okay, I'm kidding," Sabrina agreed. "But trust me. You don't want to be convicted, and Bastian's right. They're not really big on ignorance of magic as a defense."

"Or accidental magic as a defense," Miles added. "And since the boss man won't say, I'll tell you: you'd be looking at five to seven."

Five to seven... "Years?" My voice came out as a squeak. When Miles shrugged, I cleared my throat and said, "Tell me more about this other option."

"Close your shop and help me investigate. Sabrina and Miles aren't wrong. As the creator of the raw magic that killed Bitters, you're uniquely situated to help me find the killer."

Close my shop?

I never closed.

If I was contagious—which was almost never, because I was weirdly immune to colds and flus—I shut down candy-making operations, upped my part-timer's hours, and brought in temp help.

Twice in five years, I'd done that.

Once for food poisoning, and the second time because I'd had a funeral I had to attend in Texas. My namesake great-aunt's husband.

Aunt Sophia had threatened to disinherit me if I didn't attend. Whatever. Like I wanted her stuffed ferrets in evening attire or the lifetime membership to her favorite nude resort that she'd sworn we'd all get when she passed.

But then my cousin had threatened to send inappropriate items to my place of work if I didn't go and keep him company. Since he was a professional hockey player and lived for pranks, I didn't want to guess what he considered inappropriate.

(A package full of live insects? Probably not, he'd done it before. A huge packaging tube marked in bold as containing a dildo? Nope, he'd done that one already, as well. Edible poop chocolate? Already done, and also, boys were gross.)

Sabrina heaved a huge sigh, saving me from mentally recounting every single one of Bryson's terrible pranks. "I guess I can help out at Sticky Tricky Treats. But only if I get paid in candy."

Was she serious? "Uh..."

"Going once..."

Sabrina, who was rude, confrontational—

"Twice—"

But who listened to my order and delivered the perfect espresso.

"And—"

"Yes!" I hollered. "Thank you."

"Oh, you have so been had." Miles looked at me sadly. "She can eat her weight in chocolate and hard candies. Daily."

He received a rude gesture delivered with great enthusiasm by my new temporary employee.

"You can't do that inside my shop." Small children frequented Sticky Tricky Treats. And sweet little old ladies. And even sweeter little old men. And churchgoers. And just actual nice people who didn't make obscene gestures in the normal scope of their day.

She blinked huge, faux-innocent blue eyes at me. Those had to be fake lashes. No one had eyelashes that luxurious.

"She's pulling your leg," Bastian said. "Sabrina can be perfectly appropriate with customers when necessary. But Miles is right. She can eat a lot of candy. I'm much more careful with our sweets inventory now."

Sabrina stuck out her tongue at Bastian. "You're a terrible boss."

"Wait," I said. "We never agreed on how long this temporary arrangement will last."

"Until we catch the killer." When Bastian saw the frustration that had to be plastered across my face, he added with a small smile, "However long that takes."

If only it was Bryson's off season. I could con that turkey into babysitting my shop any July or August, so long as he had time to work out and access to a rink. But it was early October, Bryson wasn't available, and I really hoped that I still had a shop by the time we caught whoever had killed poor Mr. Bitters.

"Let's get this investigation rolling." The sooner we started, the sooner we finished...right? I pointed at Sabrina. "You and I are meeting at the shop at nine. Training on the basics so you don't blow up my shop."

She scowled. "But you don't open until ten."

Someone knew my store hours.

"I knew it!" Miles shook his head. "You're terrible. You totally volunteered so you wouldn't have to work morning shifts at Magic Beans."

She smirked at him. "I'm not working at Magic Beans at all until they close this case. Ten to six thirty every weekday and nine to four on Saturdays. My schedule is officially full, thank you very much, new head barista of Magic Beans."

"Oh. This does make me head barista." Miles gave Sabrina a long-distance high five.

Somehow, I felt like the only loser in this deal. Everyone else seemed to have gotten exactly what they wanted.

Miles: the head barista position at Magic Beans.

Sabrina: later mornings and all the candy she could eat.

And Bastian: an unpaid personal servant to run all of his crime-fighting errands.

"Ugh." I moaned. "Please don't tank the success it's taken me five years to build."

"Pfft. Run a candy shop? Easy. Piece of cake. Or should I say a piece of handmade specialty chocolate." She sighed. She actually looked just a little bit happy...for two seconds. Then she glared. "I haven't sucked at a single job yet and I don't plan on starting now, so stop your complaining, lady."

I turned to Bastian, looking for... I don't even know what. A sign that this investigation wouldn't last for months? That my shop wasn't about die a miserable death at the hands of a perpetually cranky twenty-something?

But he just arched his eyebrows.

Right, because he was a grump and didn't care about the survival of my tiny specialty shop that was my world. "Can we start now? Please?"

I wanted this investigation wrapped up as quickly as possible, preferably in less than three days, because that's how long I had before stock would start to look thin and I'd be splitting my time between acting as Bastian's investigative lapdog and making candy.

Bastian stood up and stretched. He was already tall, but with his arms outstretched, it felt like he filled the room. "All right, then."

He pulled a set of keys from his pocket and headed for the exterior door.

"Any chance you're going to tell me where we're going?" I stood to follow him and realized I had no cell phone, no wallet, nothing but a spare hanky and a few cinnamon candies stashed in my pocket.

"He's like that," Sabrina said as she planted herself behind his desk. "All silent and bossy. I used to think it was a German thing, but it's definitely not. It's just Bastian."

"We're going to meet Mr. Bitters's widow." Then he turned to Miles. "You're in charge. You should probably check on Bethann."

Miles leapt to his feet. "Why? What's up with Bethann? She was doing fine an hour ago. What do you know? Oh, man. Is she gonna quit? Bastian?"

But Bastian was already out the door.

Seeing as he was my ride, and I had no cash or cards on me—"Wait up!" I hollered after him.

5

I t's all about where the magic comes from." Bastian started talking as if we were in the middle of a conversation.

Except for the last ten minutes, we'd been riding in silence in his bright orange Crosstrek.

Bastian hadn't bothered to tell me where we were headed, but my best guess was Meridian, a suburban town to Boise.

Since I hadn't a clue what he was talking about, I said, "Sorry?"

Hands precisely at ten and two, Bastian spoke without taking his eyes from the road and his mirrors. "You asked about the difference between witches and wizards. That difference is primarily where the magic comes from."

"Oh." Well, that was a start. I watched Bastian

check his side and rear mirrors. Again. Who checked their mirrors every few seconds? Yeah, that was probably technically good driving, but who actually did it?

"No questions?"

"I was waiting for you to illuminate me. But if you want a question...do you mean where the magic comes from in a geographic sense? If your family is from Transylvania, then your magic comes from... oh, I don't know, drinking blood?"

Ew. I really hoped there weren't witches out there running around drinking blood, because...gross.

"That's unsanitary."

Thank goodness.

When he didn't elaborate, I said, "Bastian, will you please explain what you meant about the difference between witches and wizards?"

He switched lanes after checking his blind spot, hands still at ten and two, his gaze still shifting between his side and rearview mirrors. "Witch magic is emotional. Wizard magic is logical. I think we're being followed."

Emotion versus logic? Was this a Kirk versus Spock scenario? Intuition versus science? What did that mean? "Wait, someone's following us? What? Why is someone following us?"

"I don't know." Using the console, he made a

hands-free call to a number listed in his contacts as Transport and Tech.

"Bethann quit." Miles didn't bother with a greeting. "How did you know? How do you always know?"

"She was struggling with the feel of the coffee. All the signs were there, you just have to look closer."

Miles groaned.

Poor kid. Staffing issues were the worst. Although I didn't know what "the feel of the coffee" was, it did seem like something a good barista would have. Maybe it was like my candy motivation game.

Bastian tapped his thumb against the steering wheel a few times. "I need you to identify a car."

"Not right now. I'm mourning the loss of yet another employee. Couldn't she have made it through Sabrina's loan to Sticky Tricky Treats?"

"That's not how employment at Magic Beans works. You either have the feel, or you don't, and those that don't, don't tend to last. You know this, Miles, and with a little more experience, you'll catch the signs earlier." Bastian tapped his thumb against the steering wheel ten times. He hesitated, then did it ten more. "Is that enough mourning?"

I swallowed a laugh, because...really?

"No," Miles replied, "but what have you got?"

"White Honda Civic." Bastian rattled off a license plate number.

"Just a second." Miles whistled an unfamiliar tune over the tip-tapping of computer keys in the background. "Oh, look at that. You've got the merry widow on your tail. That car belongs to Delilah Bitters."

But we were going to visit Bitters's wife. What was she doing following us?

"Need anything else, boss? Because if not, I'm going to continue to mourn the loss of Bethann and the corresponding increase in my work hours until we can hire a replacement. I'm planning to mourn with excessive amounts of sugar, fat, and caffeine, in case that wasn't clear."

"We aren't hiring a replacement." Bastian spoke over Miles's sputter of indignation. "You, Miles. *You* are hiring a replacement. Welcome to head barista."

"But you never let Sabrina hire anyone."

"That's correct." Bastian continued to appear unruffled by the fact that we were being followed— and he kept his hands at ten and two and checked his mirrors. The man was a machine. "Do you think Sabrina should be allowed to meet prospective employees?"

"Oh, good point. Right. I'm on it, boss." Miles paused. "After I make myself a mocha latte."

"With extra whipped cream." Bastian's lips quirked. "Don't forget the extra whip, Miles." Then he ended the call.

Aw. Maybe Bastian wasn't the grumpiest German transplant in Boise.

"Is it weird that the woman we're on our way to see is currently following us?" I asked.

"Not particularly." Bastian's eyes narrowed. "What's interesting is the choice of car. She normally drives a bright blue Corvette."

"Flashy."

"Exactly."

"Maybe the Corvette is in the shop. It's not like she went out and bought a car so she could stalk the man who's investigating her husband's death."

For the first time since I'd gotten in the car with him, Bastian took his eyes off the road. He gave me a speculative look, then said, "It's possible that's exactly what she did."

"Uh, no. I was kidding. Ha, ha. Totally a joke, because that would be crazy, first of all. And second, no way I'd randomly guess exactly that crazy scenario if that's what's happening. Besides, wouldn't a good stalker rent or lease?"

"I wouldn't expect Delilah Bitters to be a *good* stalker."

Time to do a little stalking of my own. I did an internet search of Delilah Bitters on the off chance she had some kind of social media profile. Someone who drives a bright blue Corvette wants to be noticed, and wasn't that the point of social media?

Sure, some people used it to keep in touch, but a lot of people used it as a way to say, "Hey world, look at me."

"Gotcha, Delilah." She was definitely the second type, because she had profiles on all the major social media sites. "When did Bartholomew Bitters die?"

In all the drama of learning I was a witch, that I'd made the raw material for a magical killing curse, that I'd been inches from being charged with a serious crime I hadn't even realized I'd facilitated—I'd forgotten to ask when Bitters had been killed.

"Yesterday."

Weird. She'd updated her profile pics today, only a day after her husband's death. Each picture was a version on the same theme. She appeared in a long dark veil with only her boldly colored lips visible behind the lace.

Maybe sophisticated application of lip products was a witchy prerequisite. Delilah and Sabrina certainly had that box ticked. Me, with my occasional application of pink gloss? Not so much.

"What do you have?" He seemed grumpy that I'd discovered some tidbit about the widow without his help.

Actually, that wasn't fair. This was probably more resting Bastian face than an actual mood.

"I have a woman who's so completely grief-stricken that she's updated all her social media profiles with sexy widow profile pics." I really shouldn't judge. Shouldn't. Nope. Everyone grieved differently. No judging. "Seems really tacky."

I covered my mouth with my hand, but I was too late to hold back my zinger.

Bastian glanced at me, then his lips twitched. Facial tic? Oh, he thought that was *funny*.

"There was no love lost between the Bitterses."

"Okay. So, she's a suspect?"

He shrugged. "A witness, a suspect."

Like there was no difference. Maybe Mr. Big Bad Detective needed my help more than I'd realized. Even I knew those two weren't interchangeable.

"So you think she might have actually bought a car—*a car*—on a passing whim. Thought, I'm gonna follow that Bastian guy around in my sneaky white everyman car and see what he digs up on Big Daddy's death."

Bastian choked. Or maybe it was a laugh. Wow, definitely a laugh, though he managed to swallow most of it.

"Big Daddy?"

"Bartholomew? He had to be over a hundred with a name like that." And suddenly I was feeling very disrespectful with my comments about his name, his age, and even going so far as to give him a nickname.

"He's not, wasn't, over a hundred. It's a family

name, and he preferred it to the abbreviation. Bartholomew was not a Bart." He checked his mirrors again. "And it's quite possible she did buy the car specifically to blend in during her husband's investigation. You probably intuited as much. Witch intuition can be honed to a certain level of reliability, and a lot of witches in retail are especially good at intuiting motivation."

"Sure. I'm good at *candy* motivation. Intuiting the reason a person is in my shop and what candy might brighten their day isn't the same as intuiting the motivations of some random person I've never met. And for my motivation-guessing skills to work, I have to actually see the person."

"Fiery redhead, legs for miles, usually wears big, showy sunglasses."

Oops.

"I saw her in the Magic Beans parking lot." Worse, I'd even seen her get into a small white car with dealer plates. "Why are we driving out to Meridian when we could have just nabbed her in the parking lot?"

A faint pink colored his cheeks. The German driving machine was blushing. "I didn't see her in the parking lot. I only caught the tail when we were almost on the interstate."

Not entirely implausible. He'd walked through Magic Beans's rear exit several seconds before me.

He could have already been in his car when she left by the public entrance.

Wait a second, if he'd spotted our tail before we'd even gotten on the freeway... "Bastian, that was over ten minutes ago."

"I tried to get a look at the driver, but she hung too far back." He tipped his head as if reluctant to explain in greater detail. He must have been in a giving mood though, because he said, "I didn't want to interrupt Miles, since I knew Bethann had likely just quit."

Hmm. That was surprisingly thoughtful.

"Since you didn't see the wife at the coffee shop, how do you know she has 'legs for miles'?"

"We've met. The magic community in Boise isn't very large."

"And?" When he didn't immediately spill all of the good gossip on Delilah Bitters, I said, "What do you think of her? What do you know about her? What should I know before we interview her?"

"*I'm* interviewing her. *You're* approaching the interview with an open mind and a closed mouth. Besides, you already looked up her social media profile."

I crossed my arms and looked out the window. And yes, I was going for the full-on pout. This partnership bit the big one. No information-sharing on suspects. No witch history lesson. No sharing of personal details.

And, apparently, I was keeping my mouth shut. That wasn't offensive. Not at all.

Also, the car smelled like him: Christmas and cuddles. That was so wrong, because cuddles didn't smell like anything.

"Witch and wizard magic runs in families. That's why Miles and Sabrina were so surprised by your ignorance of our laws. You should have learned the basics from your family's mentor."

I looked up to find Bastian's blush gone, and—shocker!—his hands had drifted to a more natural position on the steering wheel.

"I'm not adopted or anything, and I'm pretty sure Mom didn't get busy with the milkman."

He tipped his head. "You're certain both of your parents are your biological parents."

"Yes, that's what I'm saying."

As American as Bastian sounded, the idioms were his nonnative tell. That and the cute accent that slipped in sometimes.

Perhaps I should try to be more literal...but where was the fun in that?

"It's rare for magic to skip several generations, but it's been known to happen. How many generations of Dorchesters are still living?"

"My great-aunt Sophia is the oldest."

"You should call her. She might be your family's mentor."

I snorted, because that was the last thing I wanted to do.

He shrugged as he signaled to exit the interstate. "Or not."

"Okay, so magic is inherited. What were you saying earlier about the head and the heart?"

"Emotion versus logic, but the head and the heart work, as well. Wizards tap into the logical self to create magic. Witches tap into the emotional self."

And my emotional self when creating the cupcake toppers and orange and brown candy sticks had been...not great.

"Oh."

"Oh?" He'd made a few turns now and hadn't consulted his GPS. We were slowly moving to the outskirts of Meridian.

"Yes, 'oh.' I've had an unpleasant epiphany, that kind of 'oh.' All of the candies you stole—"

"Confiscated as evidence," he corrected.

"Took without paying," I countered. "All of them were created under less than favorable circumstances." I cleared my throat. "I may have been in an emotionally heightened state when I made them. That is to say, hacked off."

"Hacked off...angry?" He turned into a driveway

leading to a structure that I wouldn't exactly call a house.

"Um, yeah, maybe." I eyed the massive edifice that someone considered a home. Distracted by its size and ostentation, I had some difficulty completing my thought. "Or at least very, very annoyed. So, how big is this place? And does a small army live here?"

"At a guess, ten to fifteen thousand square feet, and with the passing of Bartholomew Bitters, only Delilah and her staff are in residence."

In residence? Her "staff"? Was she a British aristocrat?

The white Civic pulled up next to us. Looked like Delilah's attempts at stealthily following the investigation had been foiled. Assuming that's even what she'd been doing.

Delilah exited her new car, which didn't leave us much time.

"What's the plan?" I asked, since Bastian wasn't offering any hint of what was about to go down.

"I've already told you the plan. I'm interviewing. You're keeping an open mind."

"That's not a plan, Bastian. That's—"

I about peed myself when the lady we were discussing tapped on my window.

Bastian rolled it down as I tried to get a handle on my racing pulse. I shouldn't have been so surprised, but she didn't even register in my peripheral vision.

Sunglasses resting on the very tip of her nose, she eyed the two of us over the top of them. "Bastian. Hello."

Her words were more flirtation than greeting; she almost purred them. And the leaning was pretty darn obvious. At least, it was when wearing a plunging V-neck blouse and paired with the intensity of her hungry gaze.

Me, she ignored.

"Are you going to invite us in?" Bastian asked in a flat tone. That man knew how to take *all* the flirt out of his words.

She paused, seeming to consider his question, then looked at me. Her nose wrinkled slightly. "No. I don't think so."

"Perhaps you'd like to explain why you were tailing us?" Bastian asked.

"Tailing you? I picked up a coffee from my favorite coffee shop and then came home. I haven't a clue what you're talking about." She leaned forward further, displaying a good amount of cleavage.

The dashing widow seemed to have a thing for Bastian.

Unfortunately, I was between the two of them, so I got an eyeful of her double Ds before I leaned back in my seat and let Bastian do exactly as he said: handle the interview.

He stepped out of the car and moved around to the passenger side. "You don't drink coffee, and you're not a regular patron of Magic Beans." He crossed his arms. "Why were you tailing us?"

Lovely man. I stayed included in the conversation and yet I didn't have another woman's assets shoved in my face.

"Bastian." Again with the purring. This lady.

Bastian returned her melting look with a hard one of his own.

She pushed her glasses back up her nose, and her posture changed. She ditched the inviting softness and stood taller. She had to be six feet in those heels. How did she even drive in them? Driving in heels was the worst.

When she spoke, her voice had lost its sex-kitten quality. "Fine. I need to know what happened, and you're not the type to share details." She removed her sunglasses. "Am I a target?"

Now that was an interesting development. And now I understood what Bastian meant when he said Delilah was both a suspect and a possible witness.

Investigating crime wasn't exactly a skill I'd developed over the years. I'd had a number of jobs before landing on candy-making, but not anything that involved, oh, crime or law enforcement, because I wasn't a cop or a criminal.

Except...that wasn't entirely true.

Not any longer. Now, due to unfortunate events, I was a little of both.

"Why would you be a target?" Bastian asked, apparently unaware of, or unconcerned with, my mini freak-out in the car.

"This." She gestured at him with the hand holding her glasses. The other had moved to her hip. "This is why I was trying to follow you. You and your nonanswers."

Bastian remained stubbornly quiet.

Good for him. Way to hold out against the possible murderer. Except...we sort of needed her to, uh, tell us things. In case she was the witness and not the suspect.

When neither of them spoke for an uncomfortably long time, preferring to glare (Delilah) and stand stoically silent (Bastian), I said, "So, uh, I'm sorry for your loss, Mrs. Bitters."

And I was, more than I hoped she would ever know. I didn't want to be known as the purveyor of the raw materials for murderous curses. Not in line with my branding. Also, I wasn't a psychopath and didn't have a death wish.

For a brief moment, the briefest, her lower lip

trembled. I only saw because she was in profile to me. She hadn't bothered to look at me as I spoke.

When she did turn to address me, there was nothing resembling grief on her face. No strong emotion at all, except perhaps triumph. "Didn't you hear? I won. I'm the fourth wife, and I get the entire estate."

Rather than judging her for that comment, I made note of three suspects.

And truly I didn't judge this time, because I did think Delilah was grieving her husband, whatever type of marriage Bastian believed them to have had.

But I couldn't dwell on Delilah and her unique ways of expressing or hiding her grief. I had a suspect list to ponder. A now three-ex-wives-deep suspect list.

Who was more likely to hate Bartholomew Bitters than his three ex-wives?

Oh, gosh, and Delilah would likely be dealing with the fallout at her husband's funeral, where she would not only be expected to perform all the duties of a widow, but where she might also be encountering those three ex-wives.

"I'm so sorry." The words slipped out, because... because I was. I wouldn't want to be her for any amount of money.

She smiled, but it was forced, and her eyes turned bright with the dampness of unshed tears.

"Thank you." She turned to Bastian. "I've altered my will so that everything goes to charity in hopes that will stave off any possible issues with the family. Feel free to spread that information freely. I've posted it to the family loop, but no telling who reads that."

Then she turned on her towering heels and left us.

Once the front door had closed behind her and Bastian was again behind the wheel, I said, "Did she just tell us that she's afraid her family is going to murder her?"

"The Bitters family," he confirmed. "We need to get a look at Bitters's will and her old will."

Three ex-wives and however many nieces, nephews, aunts, uncles, cousins, etcetera, littered both sides of the Bitters family tree... Looked like we had the beginnings of a lengthy suspect list.

Which only made my sympathy for Delilah Bitters grow. To suspect the people nearest and dearest to you of such a terrible deed, she had to feel very alone and unloved.

I sent a text to my favorite hockey-playing cousin: *Thanks for not being a money-grubbing psychopath.*

His reply: *I love you, too, you freak.*

And then I started googling the Bitters family.

6

P retty sure this isn't what Pinterest is for."
Sabrina eyed my murder tree board.

Family tree just seemed wrong, because real family shouldn't show up as murder suspects in an investigation of one of their own. Simple solution: I'd gone with murder tree instead.

"I needed a place to put all my research last night."

After he returned me to my car, Bastian told me to get my shop in order for an extended absence. I'd done some of that last night...and some research.

"Research." She blinked her ridiculously thick lashes. They had to be fake. "This is research? It's a bunch of pics you stole off social media."

"Well, yes." The Bitters family needed to learn about social media security settings. I snapped my laptop shut. "I'm not justifying my murder tree project. We only have another hour of training before Bastian picks me up."

Which was why I had my laptop with me at the store today. I was going to work on my murder tree board in the car. Seemed like a better option than lengthy silences filled only by the passing scenery.

Sabrina gestured to my point-of-sale setup. "I get all this. It's not rocket science. It's a lot like what we have at Magic Beans, except there I'm expected to make amazing coffee after I take orders and payment. Here I only have to bag the goods."

"Right. Speaking of the goods, we need to do a review of the merchandise."

"Nah." She twisted a lock of her long, almost black hair around her finger.

Panic swelled. She said she could do this. Bastian said she could do this.

"You can't work here and not be familiar with the chocolates and candies. It's a boutique store. We sell expensive, specialty candy. People expect decent customer service from a knowledgeable salesperson."

In fact, they expected exceptional service from a passionate salesperson, because Sticky Tricky Treats' patrons were accustomed to dealing with *me*.

Oh, Lord. What had I been thinking handing over my shop to her? She could never do this.

Sabrina was the antithesis of good customer service. She was going to ruin my business.

The tiny bells attached to the door tinkled merrily as a harried mom rushed in. No kids, just her, but I could tell. She had the look.

She caught me unawares, because we weren't open for another half hour. The front door shouldn't have been unlocked.

She looked at me and stopped all forward momentum. No small task, because she'd been moving at a good clip. "I know your sign said ten, but the door was open. I was hoping—"

Sabrina sailed forward from behind the counter and greeted Harried Mother with a charming smile. "How can I assist you today?"

The woman's demeanor instantly brightened. "Thank goodness. I need chocolate. A lot of chocolate. I forgot that I was signed up for dessert for my book club this evening, and this is the only time today that I can get away. You're right across the street and with work being so crazy, and the kids to pick up from school, and—"

Sabrina stopped her with a hand on her arm. "We've got this. How many people in your book club?"

"Twenty. Usually half come, but this was a good one, so I think maybe chocolate for fifteen people?"

Sabrina guided her to the chocolate counter. "Tell me about the club."

While the woman rattled on about the book of the month, the vibe of the group, and even talked about some of the individuals who regularly attended, Sabrina pulled out a box and started to gather a solid selection of chocolates for the group the woman had described.

Not inspired choices, but darn good for her first customer interaction. At least as on point as my part-time help, Lucy, who was no slouch and had worked here for a few years.

Sabrina was good. Smooth, efficient, familiar with the choices or faking it really well, and...warm. She was more than polite; she was attentive and kind.

Once she rang the customer up without any issues and the woman had left the store with a smile and a piece of chocolate to savor on the walk back to her office, I said, "That was very well done."

"You don't say. By the way, I already know the stock. You have an online store, and I'm not an idiot."

"You checked it out ahead of time."

"Well, duh. Yeah, I did."

I had the sudden urge to hug her, and instead of squashing it like a mosquito, I went with it.

Her body relaxed against mine for about point three seconds, then she said, "Okay, enough of that."

"You'll be on your own today after Bastian picks me up. Lucy's finishing up midterms, whatever that means when you're a grad student, so she won't be in until tomorrow."

"I read the email you sent me, and even if I hadn't, the schedule is posted right there." Sabrina pointed to the schedule I'd attached to the wall next to the employees-only door leading to the kitchen.

She'd read my email, studied STT's online stock, and even read the attached guidelines for handling food that I'd sent. I knew she'd read the attachment, because we used the thin disposable gloves common in the food industry. Magic Beans was a wash your hands and tongs kind of place.

"This is going to be great." Great was an exaggeration, but I thought maybe it would be okay. Maybe, with just a little luck, my entire business wouldn't collapse while I was off hunting a killer with a grumpy German wizard.

"Uh-huh." The look she gave me told me she knew exactly what I was thinking. "What's my employee discount?"

"Yeah, I don't think so."

"'K. Fair enough. We can revisit a discount after you see how amazing I am. We'll assume I'm earning the going rate for exceptional customer service representatives in a boutique candy store, so slightly higher than minimum wage. That should give me about two dozen chocolates for each full workday."

"I'm seriously paying you in candy?"

"Well, yeah. That was the deal. Except the whole all-I-can-eat thing isn't going to work for me. I just bought a really cute pair of jeans and they need to still fit when this gig ends. Hence the fancy math I just did."

I couldn't pay an employee in chocolate. That was just...just weird. "I'm not even sure that's legal."

And who could still fit into any jeans after two dozen chocolates consumed daily?

"Bastian will sort it." She waved a hand like that wasn't a problem at all. "Oh, and I'm definitely going to need access to your website credentials."

My website? Where up to thirty or forty percent of my revenue was generated on a good day?

That panicky feeling was back again.

"Relax. I'm a whiz with that stuff."

"That stuff," I muttered. Wouldn't someone who was a whiz know what "that stuff" was called?

"Online sales. I'm going to upgrade you." She narrowed her eyes. "This is nonnegotiable. Your current system is some weird, easily hackable garbage you put together yourself. Also, if you don't give me the credentials, I'll just hack into it myself." She smiled.

It was not a friendly a smile.

"Yep. I'll get you that information."

"Good. Now show me how your shipping for online orders works."

So went the remaining hour of Sabrina's training, with me vacillating between terrified she was going to be the demise of my business to tentative moments of hope that it would all be fine.

Near the end of her training, I emerged from my small kitchen to find Bastian perusing my stock. I quickly scanned the store for other customers, found none, and said, "Back off, mister. You're not stealing any more of my candy."

"I'm loaning you one of my best baristas. That should be more than enough payment for a handful of goods you couldn't sell anyway." He barely looked at me, because he appeared to be...shopping.

Unlike the last time he'd been in my shop, when I got no sense of the treat that would make him smile, this time I had a glimmer. "Dark chocolate–covered pretzels."

"Hm." He strolled to the counter, where all the chocolate wares were displayed. "A quarter pound." He directed this comment to Sabrina whose lips were twitching. Probably with the snarky words she was holding back.

Technically, Bastian was a customer, and therefore untouchable.

I approached her, gave her a side hug, and whispered in her ear, "He's still your boss. Give him hell."

She melted with dramatic flair and wiped her brow. "I thought for a second or two that I'd have to be nice." She wrinkled her nose. "To Bastian. That's just wrong."

Bastian didn't seem amused, but he also didn't seem surprised or annoyed. This appeared to be their normal dynamic.

Sabrina very carefully chose his chocolates, packaged them nicely, and handed them to him with a smile. A genuine smile. "I think you'll really enjoy these, boss."

Aww. So sweet.

"Just don't choke on them." And she was back.

"If you've antagonized each other enough, I'm ready to go." I slung my backpack strap onto one shoulder.

"I bought pretzels. I didn't antagonize." He flashed his innocent baby blues at me.

Christmas and cuddles. That feeling. There it was *again*.

And I was surrounded by the sugary sweet smells of my candy store, so it was just looking at him that made me think it. So wrong. So, so wrong.

"We ready?" I asked.

Parking in Boise was amazing, even downtown,

so we were in Bastian's Crosstrek and underway in minutes.

Not even five minutes passed before Bastian said, "Remember how I told you to keep an open mind when we interviewed Delilah Bitters?"

Such an improvement over yesterday's car ride, where I'd done all of the conversation initiating.

"I remember the part where you told me to keep my mouth shut."

He rolled his eyes.

Okay, he didn't, but I swear he wanted to. Mostly he was just checking his mirrors and focusing on driving like a responsible adult. "Did I say a word when you spoke?"

I bit my lip.

"Or even comment on the fact later when I drove you back to the shop?"

I might have made an annoyed grumbly growly sound, because he wasn't wrong. He hadn't complained. He hadn't said much of anything on the drive home. And I'd tried, repeatedly, to engage him in conversation.

That cutely awkward thing he did where he'd blurt out some weird fact about witches or wizards when it got too quiet in the car? He definitely hadn't done that on the way back into town.

"Well?" he prompted.

"That is correct, Bastian. You did tell me to keep

my trap shut yesterday, but you did not berate me when I failed to do so."

This time he definitely looked heavenward. He might even have muttered something unflattering in German. "Do you recall the difference in how she responded to you and to me?"

"That might have something to do with the fact that I bothered to offer my condolences to the woman. Her husband had died the day previous. Anyone with an ounce of compassion would do that."

"Possibly," he shrugged. "The important point is that you *meant* what you said. You were genuine."

I tried to recall what I'd said. Just that I was sorry her husband had passed. Heck, *of course* I was sorry. I'd played a part, however unwilling and unknowing, in his death.

"I need that."

"Sorry?" I'd been traveling down a path of guilt and regret and must have missed something. Stupid ex and his stupid texts, stupid neighbor and his stupid leaf war. Stupid me for making candy while under the influence of ex-boyfriend and bad neighbor–induced nasty moods.

"Your genuine responses. I need them."

"I'm not sure I understand. You want me to go around keeping an open mind and blurting out whatever pops into my head as we investigate?"

"No. I want you to keep an open mind and be genuine."

To-may-to, to-mah-to. But I wasn't going to argue with him. "Why?"

"Because I'm a wizard investigating what is most likely a witch crime."

Nope. Still not an explanation. But there was a kernel of information in there. "So we're for sure looking for a witch?"

"Most likely. While anyone with some magical ability should have seen the raw cursing magic in your candies, it would take another witch to use that raw material to form a targeted curse. Witch and wizard magic isn't usually compatible in that way."

"And by targeted curse, you mean killing curse."

"That's right." He turned down a street that I recognized from yesterday.

"Where are we going?"

"Magic Beans. After two hours training Sabrina, I'm sure you need some caffeine. Also, I want to see this murder tree you've created."

Sabrina was such a traitor. Not that I hadn't planned to share my weird creation, but I'd planned to share it on *my* timeline. When—if—it proved useful.

"She was impressed, I think. Otherwise, I doubt she'd have texted me." He tapped the steering wheel a few times. "If I would have offered my condolences to Delilah, she wouldn't have believed me."

"You did imply to me that her marriage wasn't the best. I believe the words you used were 'no love lost' between them. I'm not sure *I* would have believed you."

And there was that blush, just the faintest hint of pink high on his cheekbones. He'd done the same when he'd missed Delilah in the Magic Beans parking lot. "I may have underestimated her attachment to her husband. She's very flirtatious."

"Ah. Here's a hint for you, big guy. Some women flirt because they can. Because it's a sort of power they can wield. Or maybe because it's a part of their personality."

Bastian shook his head. He had a "does not compute" look on his face.

"I'm pretty sure Delilah falls more into the manipulating-men-with-her-wiles camp than being some kind of lighthearted, touchy, huggy person. Either way, flirting doesn't mean someone's actually interested or wants more."

"Maybe my radar is off."

"Nope. She's definitely attracted to you." Oops, and there I'd gone and crossed a line. But really, the man had to know he was a hottie.

He shrugged, looking more than a little uncomfortable. "She flirts with other men and finds other men attractive, but you think she genuinely grieves her husband."

"Women can be complicated. Heck, men, too." I eyed him suspiciously. "Are you telling me you didn't pick up on her grief yesterday?"

"I saw some evidence that she was more deeply affected than I would have expected."

"But you didn't trust it."

He nodded. "Another reason you're here." He shifted in his seat. "Sabrina normally does that part."

"Parsing whether your suspects' reactions and emotions are genuine?"

"Yes."

"So why isn't Sabrina helping you with this case?"

"Because you can do that *and* pick up any lingering traces of your own magic." He looked a little cagey.

He was leaving something out.

"You think? Even though I didn't know I'd packed those treats with a big ol' dose of cursing cooties, you think I'll spot that magic if I stumble on it?"

"Um-hm."

Definitely being cagey. But I'd run out of time. He was pulling into the Magic Beans parking lot.

This time we entered through the front door.

As I passed the threshold, I had the strangest sensation. A sort of déjà vu.

As the scent of properly roasted coffee and pastries reached my nose, I realized it was the same feeling I had when I walked into my own little shop: comfort and coziness and a sense of belonging. The emotions were familiar, the place different, hence the disjointed familiarity I'd felt.

That bubble of warm fuzziness burst when Bastian muttered what I'd guess from his tone was a German profanity.

And then I about had a heart attack when I spotted a man radiating with a deep rosy red glow.

ONCE HANNA HAD LEFT, I said, "You were saying about your family?"

"Oh, only that we're not close. My family situation can be complicated, but nothing like the Bitters family dynamic." He glanced at Hanna, behind the counter. "And I should be appreciative of them, however complicated they can be. Some people don't have any family at all."

7

B astian." I grabbed his tense arm and tried to pull him closer. I ended up pulling myself toward him.

"Hector." Bastian's tone was glacial.

Okay, that was weird. He'd only said one word, but I still felt the chill of it.

I whispered, hoping none of the patrons could hear me, "Is that man glowing? Because... we're in a *coffee shop*."

Bastian's lips twitched in an effort to break free of their master's control. The smile never emerged, but it lurked. Also, the tension in his arm disappeared.

Not that I was clinging to his arm.

Okay, maybe I was, but a glowing red man was adequate cause for concern. I let go but didn't step away.

At normal volume, giving no regard to the customers surrounding us—and Magic Beans did a much brisker trade than my boutique chocolate shop—Bastian said, "Yes, that man is glowing, and it's considered bad manners. Basically, the equivalent of a toddler's temper tantrum."

Which only made the man glow all the brighter.

The man named Hector. That name was awfully familiar.

Then it came to me. "You're the lime green Speedo guy! I didn't recognize you with all your clothes on."

A nearby customer giggled.

And poof, just like that, Hector's rosy red glow faded. He stormed to a rear door marked OFFICE, then stood impatiently waiting in front of it. After a few seconds, he said, "Well? Let me in, you..." He paused and looked at the good number of patrons watching him. Whatever he'd planned to call Bastian, it wasn't for public consumption. "Just open the door."

Which sealed the deal. I felt no remorse.

I'd just embarrassed a man on purpose. But then, what did you expect when your family posted updates of your tropical vacay on social media and tagged you wearing cringe-worthy, teeny-tiny swimsuit briefs? Worse yet, in a shade flattering to only the smallest percentage of the population. To be clear, lime green was not Hector's color.

Again, the Bitters family needed to have a look at their social media security settings.

Or, here was a revolutionary concept, don't post pictures you find embarrassing for the world's viewing pleasure.

Alternatively, Hector could have owned that lime green Speedo choice, and my attempt at embarrassing him wouldn't have worked. But that wasn't the kind of guy Hector was, and I'd intuitively known that.

Bastian strolled—he made it that obvious he was in no hurry—to his office door, then paused and looked at Hector as if he were a bug. That was a skill I wouldn't mind acquiring. I'd wield it as my weapon of choice every time a solicitor ignored my very clearly worded sign warning them away.

Hector stepped aside, giving Bastian more room.

I'm not sure what I expected. Hand waving? An incantation? Some kind of magic, certainly, because otherwise Hector would have just opened the door himself.

But, nope. Bastian put his hand on the doorknob, twisted, and pushed the door open. Then he gestured for Hector and me to enter.

I walked into a familiar room. It was just as I remembered: the tidy desk with the sleek laptop, the blue rug Sabrina was fond of, the sofa that had cradled my aching head after Miles had shipped me from Sticky Tricky Treats to here with his magic beam-me-up-Scotty witch technology. Apparently, I hadn't been that out of it after my magical transport.

Since Bastian was likely to sit behind his desk, I removed my coat and took a seat at the end of the couch closest to the desk, leaving the awkwardly placed and seemingly uncomfortable chair in front of Bastian's desk for Hector. It was that or the two armchairs that were much further away and threatened to swallow their occupants.

Bastian gestured for Hector to sit, before carefully draping his coat along the chair that sat behind the desk.

"I'll stand," Hector said, as if that would give him an advantage.

Unlikely. He seemed the sort to be perpetually at a disadvantage.

He also seemed the sort to disdain chocolate-eaters and candy-lovers. In other words, not my kind of people.

Bastian merely inclined his head in an "as you wish" kind of way and sat. "I assume there's a reason you've come to my place of business and made a spectacle."

A spectacle *of yourself* was implied.

"Just because you have ice water running in

your veins, wizard, that's no reason to criticize those of us with actual feelings. My brother is dead."

Oh, and now I felt bad. I'd put the murder tree together, but I hadn't had a lot of time to study the connections between the family members.

But then that comment: ice water. I hadn't known Bastian long, but he was a teddy bear compared to the vibes I was getting from temper-tantrum-throwing Hector.

"You haven't spoken to your brother in over a decade. Was there a recent reconciliation of which I'm unaware?"

And that dissolved the remaining twinges of guilt. Thank you, Bastian. Also, he'd told me to keep an open mind and to go with my gut. My gut didn't like this guy. It also wasn't doing somersaults and pointing at him as the murderer—but an intuitive organ can only do so much, and that likely exceeded reasonable expectations of it.

"You know there hasn't been." Hector's face turned a reddish, purplish shade.

He was awfully angry for a guy who had magic. As a newbie witch, I felt vulnerable to his aggression. I was one of the magical crowd but without any of the knowledge or training.

I didn't want to get squished flat by a murderer's magic if I could avoid it—or even the magic of a

magenta-faced,   sometimes-lime-green-Speedo-
wearing witch with the self-control of a toddler.

For now, I'd just have to rely on the kindness of
strangers—or, at least, the kindness of the ICWP and
its local members—to keep me safe.

"Again, I ask, why are you here?" Bastian might
not have ice in his veins, but he did manage to retain
a calm demeanor, like a grown-up adult person does,
in the face of unsolicited conflict.

Hector's response was delayed by a knock at the
office door.

Bastian called out, "Enter."

A timid mouse of a woman let herself in carrying
a tray with three drinks. She proceeded to deliver
drinks we hadn't ordered.

I thanked her when she handed me a mug, but I
also reevaluated my split-second first impression.

She was thin, taller than average, with medium
brown hair, brown eyes. Her demeanor was
subdued, which I'd mistaken as timid at first glance.
And she was no mouse. If you looked, really looked,
she was gorgeous. The kind of beauty that might be
quiet if it wasn't highlighted with mascara and lip
gloss, but it was there in her bones and her skin.

Interesting. I glanced at her name tag as I took
my first sip. Perfect.

"Thank you, Hanna."

She didn't make eye contact—although she came

close, aiming perhaps for my left earlobe?—and murmured, "You're welcome."

I sipped my perfectly prepared light roast with a generous helping of macadamia milk as she handed Bastian a black coffee and Hector...an herbal tea.

It figured the man would be in a place that served heavenly coffee and his perfect drink would be an herbal tea.

And I didn't doubt that it was his perfect drink, because our shy barista had nailed mine even though my last drink here had been something entirely different. My morning, afternoon, and evening caffeine needs varied. I wasn't exactly a caffeine snob. It was simply a question of chemistry and sleeping habits.

And also, maybe I was a little bit of a caffeine snob.

Hanna hurried out the door once the last drink was delivered.

Shy, yes, but she probably had a better chance at making it at Magic Beans than her predecessor Bethann, who'd lacked the much sought after "feel" for coffee, according to Bastian.

The elusive "feel" seemed to cause Magic Beans ongoing staffing issues, so maybe Hanna with her special touch would put an end to the revolving door of baristas at what I suspected was going to become my favorite coffee shop in Boise.

"That evil witch did it. She murdered my brother." Hector's color wasn't looking too good. The excited flush of an overexcited man, not the magical glow he'd been sporting earlier. The man looked like he was on the cusp of a medical event. Stroke, heart attack, passing out from excessive ill humor?

Also, I really hoped I'd heard him correctly, and he'd called someone an evil witch and not the other word that sounded very similar.

Bastian might toss around a profanity or two, but in German and not actually aimed at a particular person. I might even let the occasional naughty word pass my lips. But Hector's words carried the weight of intent, nasty intent. My gut was telling me that Hector had a mean streak broad enough to be a little scary in a person who could practice magic.

"Who are you referring to?" Bastian sipped his coffee.

"You know who. Your prime suspect. The only person you've bothered to interview so far." He paused long enough to shoot a judgmental look at me that was tinged with a hint of creepy-old-pervyman. "When you weren't busy getting up to who-knows-what with your new girlfriend."

That feeling you get when you've been on a transatlantic flight, when your seat neighbor coughed the entire flight and the flight attendant spilled a drink on you because some idiot tried to pass her in the aisle at the exact moment she was handing you your drink? As if your skin is covered in a layer of filth and germs and a stickiness that cannot be wiped away? That's how I felt after one lingering look from Hector.

But I kept my mouth shut. Not because Bastian had explained my role as the primarily silent partner, but because my gut said it was a good idea.

This man had an agenda. He was here for a reason, and I didn't think it was remotely rooted in a desire for justice. And if me being quiet for a few minutes resulted in him revealing that agenda, then I'd keep my mouth shut.

"You know English isn't my first language. Best to speak plainly."

I worked on my poker face. As if Bastian had any issues understanding purple-faced Hector. Please. For some reason, Bastian wanted Hector to accuse Delilah in plain English.

"That...that woman. That money-grubbing whore of a wife of his, Delilah. She killed my brother."

"Liar." The word was past my lips before I'd even registered the underlying certainty with which I spoke. I guess I wasn't keeping my mouth shut after all.

Hector was not pleased.

I wasn't particularly pleased myself. I didn't

normally go around telling people they were full of it. First, I'm not a particularly confrontational person. And second, how would I even know?

But after examining him and my feelings, I was even more certain. "He's lying, Bastian. He has no confidence in that statement whatsoever. Why would you lie about that? Why accuse her if you don't think she did it?"

Hector's jaw trembled with his fury. He didn't bother to answer me.

"Hector doesn't inherit under the current will. Delilah inherits everything." Bastian kept his cool, even when facing a ticking time bomb of an opponent.

Neat trick. One I envied. I could feel my heart rate increasing and knew from past experience (my ex-boyfriend came to mind) that I sometimes said and did regrettable things when faced with a volatile and unreasonable human being, especially one intent on lying.

But not Bastian. He was still calm. Unruffled by Hector's glares or the visible signs of his wrath.

It was almost as if the more Hector lost control, the greater Bastian's became.

If that was a spell, I wanted it. Wizard magic or no.

Turning my attention back to the puzzle of Hector's accusation, some of the pieces fell into place. "If she's convicted of murdering him, she can't inherit."

"She should never have inherited anyway. The bulk of Bartholomew's estate is family money. It should stay in the family."

I'd been spot-on with that murder tree concept. This guy might not deserve a spot in Bartholomew's family tree, but he was a great addition to the murder tree.

Poor Delilah. If this was the garbage she was dealing with, I could see why she thought she'd be targeted.

"Well?" Hector leaned forward in his chair. "What are you doing about it? You talked to her for maybe two, three minutes. You didn't even question her properly, and you should have been arresting her."

The man was spitting mad. As in, he spat as he spoke.

I leaned as far away from him as possible.

As if the spitting and general malevolence weren't enough, he wasn't drinking his tea. He'd abandoned it on Bastian's desk. Someone gives you a drink, at least pretend that you like it. Maybe that wasn't good manners; maybe that was a personal quirk. Regardless, I was underwhelmed by Hector in all ways.

So underwhelmed that I was having difficulty

seeing him as a mastermind behind his brother's death. And with Delilah as the current beneficiary, the murder of his brother would certainly have required some masterminding. He'd have to have killed his brother in a way that implicated Delilah, and also ensured that the funds he clearly so desperately wanted came to him.

Also, unless he was a fabulous actor, he didn't have a clue who I was. Bastian's *girlfriend*? Not last I checked, Mr. Bitters. I wasn't his girlfriend; I was his extorted crime-solving free labor. The woman paying penance for having created the raw material of the curse that killed Bartholomew. Raw material it was seemingly increasingly likely that Hector did *not* use to kill his brother.

I realized Bastian was waiting for some indication from me. I shook my head slightly, hoping that conveyed my belief that he wasn't the guy.

"As a member of the deceased's immediate family, you'll be informed of the outcome of the investigation. Unless you'd like to share any actual evidence against Delilah Bitters, you may leave."

You may leave.

Bastian just dismissed the near apoplectic man like he was a naughty child called before the principal.

I wanted to pat him on the back. Mostly because I didn't like Hector one little bit.

Guilt nagged, because whether he'd been estranged from his sibling or not, the man had still lost a close relative.

As he stood in a huff, I said, "I'm sorry about what happened to your brother. It was a terrible thing."

All true. I didn't offer sympathy over his loss, because I wasn't entirely sure he felt any sorrow over losing his brother...only his brother's money.

His gaze skated over me, once again making me feel dirty, and then he stormed out of the office, closing the door with the force of an enraged teenage girl.

"Wow. Are all witches so melodramatic?" I asked after the sound of the slammed door had faded. Legit question, because I'd gotten strong melodrama vibes from Delilah, as well. "And how about the sleaze quotient? He was a seven or eight, easily."

"Miles and Sabrina are witches."

I considered his reply as I sipped and enjoyed my coffee. "True. Miles is nothing like the Bitters family. Sabrina..." Actually, neither was Sabrina. She had a certain flair, but it was more of a sharp edge than overblown posturing. "Good point. So it's just the Bitterses."

"No, there are certainly witches who choose to embrace their inner child—"

I choked, and almost snorted coffee out of my nose. "That is not what that phrase usually means."

He took a sip of his coffee, an amused light glinting in his eyes.

"Which you know very well. Hey, you mentioned the will. Did you get a copy of it?"

He nodded. "All of them, actually. Very straight-forward. Everything to Delilah. What was interesting, however, was that she was the first wife set to inherit the entirety of his estate."

Delilah's words rang in my head. "I win. She said, 'I win.' I thought she was being intentionally crass about the fact that she was the only wife to have outlived her husband."

"None of them were ever included in Bartholomew's previous wills beyond token amounts, and they were completely removed once divorce settlements had been made."

That was...odd. "Do you think he left them out because of what Hector said? Because most of his wealth was inherited and he thought it should stay in the family?"

Bastian kicked back in his chair. "No. None of the wills left significant bequests to family members. Maybe it was his way of ensuring the women marrying him weren't just there for the money."

I wasn't sure exactly why else they would be. Oh,

ouch. That was incredibly mean spirited, especially after witnessing Delilah's genuine grief firsthand.

"Whatever the reason he excluded them, it couldn't have made any of them feel good. So I guess we have three ex-wives with motive? Assuming revenge is any kind of motive."

Bastian raised his eyebrows. I took that to mean that revenge was a solid reason for murder in the witch world. "We have one, perhaps two ex-wife suspects. One of Bartholomew's wives is dead. Another is living abroad, though I've got Miles checking that she's still in France. That leaves one suspect living locally with a motive for revenge."

I swallowed the last of my coffee. No to-go cup, so I figured best to finish up before we walked out the door to check out our only local ex-wife. I stood up. "Okay then. Let's go meet this ex."

"No. Let's have a look at this murder tree of yours first."

I swallowed a groan. I wasn't excited to share my hodgepodge of miscellaneous stolen social media pics. Well, that wasn't entirely true. I did want to point out a particular lime-green-brief-clad jerk, just for grins.

Miles busted into the office through the door to the parking lot. "Bastian. You'll never believe—" He leaned over, grabbed his knees, and panted.

Bastian tapped his finger on his desk. Ten times. And then ten again. "I'll never believe what?"

Miles lifted a finger in a classic just-one-second gesture. He did look awfully red in the face.

"Is he going to be okay?" I wouldn't have pegged Miles as a hardcore workout nut, but he also hadn't seemed out of shape...until now.

Bastian blinked slowly. "Miles lives around the corner. I'm assuming he ran from his apartment instead of calling for some unknown reason. But yes. He's a twenty-six-year-old man in good health. He'll be fine. I'll be sure to start taking him on my short runs after we've resolved this case."

Miles lifted his head with a panicked look at Bastian. "No. Not gonna happen." Gasp. "And check your phone. I called." Gasp. "The second wife is dead. Murdered."

Bastian frowned, then pulled his phone from his pocket. "I was in the middle of something."

I replied to Miles's questioning look, "Hector Bitters threw a temper tantrum. You just missed him." Directing my question to Bastian, I asked, "Which wife is the second one?"

"The witch living abroad, Cammi. If she was still in France... Miles?"

Miles shook his head. "Back in the states. Seattle." He looked less red, more a sweaty pink color.

I scrunched up my nose. "You really should get a little more exercise, Miles."

"I exercise." He looked awfully offended for a guy whose recovery time resembled that of an asthmatic man three times his age with a video game addiction.

"When was she killed?" Bastian asked.

"That's why I was in a rush. Tuesday, boss. Hit and run."

Only a day before Bartholomew, and Seattle was just a hop, skip, and a short plane ride from Boise.

Bastian muttered a word in German that I was fairly certain was profane.

Which made sense, because... "We have to get to the third ex. She has no idea what's going on." Unlike Delilah, who was at least on guard against evil acts.

"Yes," Bastian agreed as he stood and grabbed his coat. "You've tried to reach her?"

Wide-eyed, Miles said, "Yeah. No luck. Another reason I sprinted here hoping to catch you."

"Call Delilah Bitters." He shrugged into his jacket. "Tell her what's happened to Cammi."

"I'll text you Melanie Hampton's address, Boss!" Miles hollered.

But he was talking to Bastian's back as he exited the office to the parking lot.

Once again, I found myself running to catch up with Bastian for fear I'd be left behind.

It didn't occur to me until I was in his car and securing my seat belt that a normal person might actually *want* to miss whatever happened next.

A confrontation with an embittered ex...or worse, the discovery of her dead body.

8

I was starting to see a pattern to Bastian's finger and thumb tapping.

After ten taps with his thumb on the steering wheel, he redialed Melanie Hampton's number. He'd already tried four times with no result.

Thumb and finger tapping were Bastian's crutch for patience. If I wasn't so worried about ex-wife number three, I'd probably find it endearing.

Boise might be the largest city in Idaho, but unlike cities in Texas, it had no major through roads. No loop that swooped around the entirety of the city, no interstate that traveled through its heart, no highway running along the edge of town. With the exception of a short strip that locals called the connector, if you traveled in town, you drove on roads with a plethora of stoplights and stop signs. Boise was an entire city of neighborhood streets.

Our journey to Melanie Hampton's home, a mere three miles away, took a total of fifteen minutes and that was with almost no traffic.

Fifteen minutes of finger tapping and redials.

If that wasn't a clear sign that Bastian was concerned for Ms. Hampton's well-being, then his insistent knocking on her door once we arrived sealed it.

Unlike Hector Bitters, I didn't see Bastian as a man with ice in his veins. A man with an even temper who kept his cool in stressful situations? Yes, that man I saw.

Just not right now.

When the pounding of his open palm on Ms. Hampton's door yielded no results, Bastian started in with his fist.

I touched his shoulder, and he stopped. "If she was home, she'd have heard you the first ten times."

He stepped back and pinched the bridge of his nose.

No, there definitely wasn't any ice water in his veins.

I rubbed his arm. "Just because she's not answering her door, that doesn't mean that anything has happened to her. She could be traveling. Gosh, she could be at a hair appointment, for all we know."

He gave me an intent look. "Is that what you think? That she's got a hair appointment?"

"What? No. I mean, I don't know." I frowned at him. "Quit doing that. I don't have any weird vibes telling me she's out for a trim. I'm just saying, there's probably a mundane explanation for her absence. Something other than murder and mayhem."

"Maybe." But he looked calmer as he walked to her garage.

"And maybe Cammi's murder is a coincidence." Not that I believed that, but I also couldn't think of a reason a murderer would target Bitters's ex-wives.

"Isn't there some magic you can do? Something to track her location?" I trailed behind him as he peered into her garage through the glass in the door.

"Her car is gone." He stepped away from the door and retrieved his phone from his pocket. "Miles, can you— No, she's not here. I need you to —" He blinked slowly. "Yes, Hanna does seem to have the feel. Could you—" An impatient expression crossed his face. "Yes, Miles. You did a fantastic job hiring her." He paused, the index finger of his left hand tapping against his cargo-pants-clad thigh. All that hotness and then...cargo pants.

Finally, Miles slowed the flow of his words long enough for Bastian to say, "Can you do a little digging into Melanie Hampton's schedule? Her plans for the weekend, where she's spending money, that sort of thing." After a pause, he said, "That's fine," then ended the call.

When Bastian saw the expression on my face, he shrugged. "He must have chugged a few cold brews after we left."

That explained it. Cold brew coffee had a higher concentration of caffeine than many other coffee products. What that boy should have been chugging was water. He needed a keeper.

"To answer your earlier question," Bastian said, "magic doesn't work like that. Much of it requires proximity or even touch. Failing that, then a great deal of preparation."

"Like Miles tagging you in advance so he can transport you in a hurry."

"That's right." He wandered around the exterior of Melanie's house in a suspicious manner that was bound to have the nosiest neighbors reporting on their neighborhood app, or worse, calling the police.

"Could you try looking a little less like a burglar casing the joint? Peering into her windows in broad daylight is going to get us questioned by the cops."

He glanced my way and frowned, then continued to peer suspiciously into her kitchen window. "Nothing looks amiss inside."

"No dead bodies lying around waiting to be discovered?" I was kidding, but I still held my breath until he replied.

"No. And no signs of a struggle."

"That's good news, at least."

And then it all went south. An elderly woman walking a dog stopped in front of Melanie's house. I couldn't think of her as Ms. Hampton if I was familiar enough to be peeking through her curtains.

I feigned partial blindness in hopes Melanie's nosy neighbor would continue walking, but that tactic failed when she hollered, "Hello."

Before turning to address her, I glared at Bastian. "Hello," I replied in a much friendlier tone than the other woman had used. "How are you doing today?"

"That depends. What's your interest in Mel's place?" Both her and her little terrier gave me the evil eye.

I jabbed an elbow into Bastian's rib cage hard enough to elicit a grunt. "I told you," I whisper-yelled. Wild guess, this was not one of those times I should keep my mouth shut. I smiled at Melanie's neighbor. "We're trying to get in touch with Melanie. My friend and I have some news for her, and it's important we talk to her as soon as possible."

"What kind of news?" she asked, not relenting with the hairy eyeball one little bit.

"The bad kind," Bastian replied.

The woman turned her attention to Bastian, though the dog kept his stare directed at me. "It's to do with that rotten cheating ex of hers, isn't it? The one who died recently."

Bastian and I shared a glance. How did she even know the man was dead?

"Don't look that way. You'll read the obits daily when you're my age, too."

If I made it to her age, maybe I would. My recent introduction to the magical crowd hadn't inspired confidence in our longevity.

"It does, in fact, have to do with Bartholomew Bitters's death," Bastian replied. "Do you happen to know if Ms. Hampton is expected home soon?"

She gave Bastian a piercing look. After several seconds of scrutiny, she said, "Oh, all right then. She's in the mountains with her gentleman friend for a long weekend. If the news can wait, she'll be back on Sunday." She pursed her lips, clearly considering her next words. "Mel works hard, and she doesn't take much time off. If you don't have to ruin her weekend, please don't."

Which is the point at which I considered the house whose windows we'd been peering inside.

It was a well-maintained but modest home. And small. Unless Melanie Hampton's home had magical properties like the Tardis in *Dr. Who*, with an interior larger than the exterior, then I'd guess it to be no more than a thousand square feet.

In comparison to the widowed Mrs. Bitters, who

lived in a building large enough to house a hockey team.

What kind of settlement had Bitters's exes received? His third ex-wife worked so hard even her neighbor knew about it. And while her home was adorable, it was so far removed from the grandeur of the current Mrs. Bitters's home as to be in a different world.

Maybe she loved her work.

Maybe she'd frittered away her settlement.

Maybe she'd invested it and had a nice nest egg.

The possibilities were endless. But I couldn't help thinking that perhaps Mr. Bitters had been stingy in his divorce settlements. He'd been the man with the money, capable of hiring the best attorneys and spending whatever time and money was necessary to ensure his exes walked away with exactly what he wanted. There was also the possibility of an unfavorable prenuptial agreement.

I looked up to find that Bastian had handled the nosy elderly neighbor, and both she and her dog were departing.

"Sorry. I was just thinking about motives and such."

He arched an eyebrow. "Motives and such?"

"Yes. The differences between the two women's lifestyles and how that might be a motivation for murder."

"You're seeing Melanie Hampton as more of a murder suspect than a potential victim."

Was I? That didn't feel right. I shrugged.

"She can be both," Bastian said. "She *is* both."

"Well, I don't find that helpful. I'd like to have fewer suspects. Actually, I'd like no suspects and one killer. A killer who's arrested and safely locked away, so I can return to Sticky Tricky Treats and my life of candy-making."

Except that wasn't exactly our deal. Our deal was to find the killer. "Find" could mean simply to discover the identity of our killer. But I wanted him or her in cuffs, behind bars, tucked away from the world of people who were just trying to get by day to day with our regular non-murdery lives.

I scrubbed my hands across my face. "This is stressful."

"Hmm. We have to warn her. Vacation or not. Suspect or not. With any luck, Miles will find a digital trail shortly and will be able to give us her current location."

Bastian headed back to his car, so I trailed behind. "And if he can't find a digital trail?"

"*Then* we'll use magic."

As Bastian drove back to Magic Beans, where I'd left my laptop in my rush to catch up with my fleeing driver, I talked through my thoughts about Melanie Hampton. "She's out of town. That's good. Maybe she'll be safer out of town. If she's not the killer." I tacked on the qualifier at the last second.

It was interesting, but I wasn't thinking about Melanie as a killer. Or even as a suspect. I was thinking of her purely as a potential victim. "Do you want to know my impressions even if they're based on...well, on nothing?"

Bastian agreed, without hesitation, that yes, he did want my impressions regardless of how they came about.

When I didn't immediately spill the entire contents of my churning mind, he said, "What are you thinking?"

"That Hector is a four-letter word my mom wouldn't be pleased to hear me use, but not his brother's killer."

He nodded. Not in agreement so much as a signal to keep talking.

So I did.

"And Melanie, I just don't see it: her killing her ex. How long ago did their marriage end? Because she's already dating a man she takes on long weekend trips. And I bet you saw the twinkle in the nosy neighbor's eyes when she mentioned Melanie's 'gentleman friend.' The neighbor likes him. So either he's around a good bit or Melanie talks about him a lot, otherwise I doubt she'd have an opinion at all."

"Anything else?"

"The house was weird."

He raised his eyebrows at that.

"Okay, weird is the wrong word. It was so... middle class."

"Which means what exactly?"

"What it means is that Melanie Hampton could be *my* neighbor. I could run into her at my grocery store. She might bank at my bank. If that's where she lives... It makes her seem so, well, normal."

"Ah. Unlike Delilah Bitters."

"Yes! Exactly. It's weird. Delilah is the fourth wife, Melanie the third, and yet they're so different. It makes me wonder what the other two wives were like."

"Rachael, his first wife, died before I moved to the area. Miles should have some kind of file put together on her later today or tomorrow. He'll have started working on it already. That's probably how he discovered that Cammi, the second wife, had been murdered."

"Did you know Cammi?" I asked.

"Yes." His reply lacked inflection.

"And...?"

"And she wasn't a pleasant sort of woman. She was beautiful." He paused, tapped the steering wheel ten times with his thumb, then said in a much more normal tone, "She was a beautiful but unkind woman."

"Did you date?" Because his responses indicated some type of familiarity beyond the superficial.

"No. She was with a friend of mine for a few months. She left him worse than she found him." He glanced at me, but then his eyes were right back on the road and his mirrors. "I'm sure Miles will have a thorough file on her, as well."

Left him worse than she found him? That sounded ominous.

I dithered over whether to push for more information, but Bastian ended my internal debate when he began speaking.

"Look, she wasn't evil, just self-absorbed. Gorgeous, fun, and terribly selfish. Stefan, my friend, is an easygoing guy. He comes from money, doesn't need to work, but he enjoys his job. He's a professor at a university. Cammi came into his life like a whirlwind. She dragged him to parties, tried to pull him into a lifestyle he wasn't suited to. He was so enthralled by her that he followed blindly. He damaged his career trying to make her happy, and she just laughed. Said he didn't need the money, so why did he care?"

Love could sometimes turn people into idiots. Case in point, my ex Bryan. And it sounded like Bastian's friend Stefan had been a level-seven or -

eight idiot, but that didn't make how Cammi had treated him any better.

"I'm really sorry."

"Yeah. He's a good person, and she used him for his money and his family's connections."

"How does a woman like that land in Idaho? Boise doesn't seem like a natural fit for a social-climbing beauty intent on bagging a wealthy man."

"Stefan's family is influential in the magical community. She was blacklisted in Europe, which was probably why she settled for someone like Bartholomew. They met on a business trip to Germany, and she followed him back. He was divorced shortly thereafter, and then married within months."

This was the first I'd heard, however tangentially, of Bastian's life before Boise. There was one interesting point that he'd unintentionally revealed. Either his friend was a wizard who'd dated a witch, or he was friends with a witch.

Unlike Miles and Sabrina, who could be dismissed as colleagues, he'd clearly labelled Stefan a friend. The question of wizards and witches and whether the two comingled in a social sense had been burbling in the back of my mind since I'd learned that Bastian belonged to one camp, while I belonged to the other.

Not that it mattered, because it wasn't as if I wanted to *socially mingle* with Bastian.

Probably.

At least, not now, in the middle of a murder investigation.

I let that thought fade away, and concentrated on the passing scenery, because truly, me and romance weren't the best of friends, and thoughts to the contrary needed to stay very buried.

It occurred to me as we pulled into the Magic Beans parking lot several minutes later that my motivation to participate in this investigation had changed significantly in a short time. I was no longer driven by a desperate desire not to rot in witch prison for the next five to seven years.

Primarily because I didn't think Bastian would let that happen. Bastian righted wrongs, and me ending up in prison would be very, very wrong. He may have felt pressured by his rule-following personality to arrest me, and he may have needed a push from Miles and Sabrina to look for an alternative to charging me with a terrible crime, but in the end, he'd given me an alternative.

One that I was grabbing with both hands, and not just because I didn't fancy a prison sentence.

Someone had taken my candy and used it to *murder* another human being.

My candy that was infused with *my* magic.

I might not have fully understood how magic worked, but I was getting the gist, and I did know that it was intensely personal.

It was as if someone had reached inside me and stolen my very feelings...then turned around and used them for a terrible purpose.

Bastian had given me more than an alternative to prison. He'd given me a chance to both take back my power after a sort of violation, and he'd given me a chance to make the wrong done with my magic, if not right, then a little better.

9

Bastian and I reviewed my murder tree, but we did it in the customer area of the coffee shop, in the two overstuffed armchairs tucked away in the quietest corner.

We'd walked into the office to find a highly caffeinated Miles typing frantically on Bastian's laptop. He hadn't even shifted his gaze from the screen when we opened the office door. He'd just pointed at the door and said, "Out."

Bastian hadn't shown an ounce of irritation over the perfunctory command or the fact that his desk had been usurped.

He'd guided me back out of the office with a hand on my lower back, and murmured, "He's in the zone. He's rude when he's like this, but very, very productive."

In the space of twenty minutes, between Bastian's phone call to him and now, Miles had changed from a highly caffeinated chatterbox to a hyperfocused research machine. In the zone, indeed.

While Bastian scrolled through the pictures and names that I'd pulled from social media and pinned to my murder tree board, I asked about the wills. "I've been wondering: how did you get access to Bitters's previous wills?"

"Ah." He looked up from the laptop resting on the ottoman placed between us. "Delilah mentioned a family group email list, so I had Miles hack it."

It took me a few seconds to process what that meant. "Bitters posted each variation of his will on a group email list that included his family members?"

No. That couldn't be right, because that was beyond odd. It was... Actually, words failed.

"And not just his close family. The Bitters family email group includes a rather extensive collection of extended family."

"Was he *trying* to make his family angry?" Because why else would he share a will that excluded his family from inheriting what Hector had claimed was originally family money?

"I believe it was more about manipulation." He snapped my laptop shut. "Thanks, that was helpful. Like a snapshot of the family, it firmed up some impressions I had."

I smiled. I was glad my little foray into the social side of investigation had been helpful. "So how did posting his will help him to manipulate his family if he cut them out?"

"He'd include small bequests and then remove them. I can only assume based on his most recent interactions with those family members."

I wrinkled my nose. "That gives every single person mentioned and removed a motive."

Bastian shook his head. "Not a very good one. His practice of adding and removing individuals was practically commonplace, so why now? And no one except Delilah benefitted from the latest will, so there's no financial gain. Why not wait? Let Delilah fall out of favor, see who was added back into the will over time."

"I guess?"

"You don't agree."

"I'm just not sure. Nothing really stood out when I created the murder board. And even if one of the beneficiaries of an old version of the will was angry enough to kill, how does that tie into Cammi's death? We're missing something about the family."

"With any luck, Miles's background research will reveal information that will help us to understand a connection between the motives for the two murders. This family." Bastian shook his head. "The whole experience of reading through the documents was unpleasant. My family situation is—" He smiled up at Hanna, who had thoughtfully brought us refills.

"Half-caff," she murmured as she handed me a mug. My earlier drink had been fully caffeinated, but she'd scored another ten of ten from me, because I was ready to start winding my caffeine consumption down a little.

Bastian drank his dark roast black. Morning, noon, and night, so far as I could tell.

Once Hanna had left, I said, "You were saying about your family?"

"Oh, only that we're not close. My family situation can be complicated, but nothing like the Bitters family dynamic." He glanced at Hanna, behind the counter. "And I should be appreciative of them, however complicated they can be. Some people don't have any family at all."

His phone pinged with a text. He retrieved it from one of his many pockets. After a quick glance, he nodded. "Cammi's hit-and-run has been officially tied to the magic community. There are some inconsistencies with witness statements and some technology glitches that, when combined, indicate magical interference."

"Definitely magical, but not necessarily connected to Bitters's murder?"

"No connection has been made," he agreed. "Yet."

I frowned. "There's no way my candy could have had anything to do with her death, right?"

Because that would definitely connect the two. And there was no reason a murderous nutter *wouldn't* have used the same means twice. Have candy; will travel. The stuff was highly portable and would be no problem on a plane.

"Bitters died after consuming a potion. We know definitively that's not how Cammi died." Bastian paused, and his eyes squinted a bit as he watched me. After several seconds, he said, "Some of the cursed candies are unaccounted for, so the killer could have more in reserve. The two candy sticks that you told me were missing from your inventory, for example. And the killer didn't necessarily use the entirety of the cupcake topper in the potion used to kill Bitters."

Those two missing candy sticks...

After looking at my initial inventory for the cursed items, I'd discovered only one cupcake topper and two orange and brown candy sticks gone. It looked like someone had paid cash for the cupcake topper—during one of Lucy's shifts, because I'd have remembered selling it—and that someone had shoplifted the candy sticks.

I nodded numbly.

Confronting the realities of my involvement in a man's death took my breath away. And I didn't see the impact lessening any time soon.

But it was all fine. So far as anyone knew, my candy hadn't been a part of ex-wife number two's murder.

"Lina?" I looked down to find my hand clasped in Bastian's.

Maybe I wasn't so fine. I had, after all, created candy that held raw cursing magic inside its sugary soul.

I knew which events had triggered the cursing of my candy, but when I examined them, they were so very small. Little blips of discontent in my life. Nothing so large as to have created magic that could *kill* a person.

But then, it hadn't been about the stupid texts from my boyfriend. Or the ridiculous neighbor and his vendetta against me and the leaves blowing into his yard from my tree.

I'd been disappointed in mankind. Both times, I'd been overwhelmed by the petty vindictiveness of people in general. And it was that feeling—my temporary disenchantment with the human race—that had resulted in my cursed candies.

"I'm sorry. I was just remembering the whole silly chain of events leading up to the creation of the cupcake toppers." I let go of his hand.

He didn't seem put out by the overfamiliarity. Then again, he wasn't always easy to read, like that first time he came into the shop and ended up arresting me.

"The timing of everything strikes me as interesting." Bastian spoke lightly, as if I hadn't just squeezed the blood from one of his extremities. "Why obtain the means for creating the edible curse and then not use it for weeks?"

We'd both had a look at the timing, and Lucy had been working very little of late—midterms—so after consulting her, we decided that the topper had been purchased two or more weeks previous.

Buying and not using... Hmm. "A planning period?"

"Yeah." He pulled out his phone and sent a text. It pinged with a reply almost immediately. "Cammi only arrived in Seattle two days before she was killed."

"Did you just text Miles, who is sitting ten feet away from you?"

Bastian grinned. "He told us to get out. I'm complying and minimizing the disturbance to his process." His grin faded. "But the important point here is that, if the two murders are connected, then Cammi's return to the States triggered the sequence of events that are now in motion."

"What if the purchase of the cupcake topper was

the beginning of all this? The killer must have walked into my store, unknowing that the equivalent of a gun was being sold inside. They saw the topper, recognized its potential, bought it, and then began planning."

"No."

I blinked, pulled from what was looking to be a nice guilt spiral.

"Whoever did this could have killed Bitters using their own magic. You might have made it a little easier—*a little*—but it's not as if we don't all have access to lethal magic of our own. Combining another person's magic might have made it easier for the killer, but it wasn't the deciding factor."

"Good to know," I said over a lump in my throat. "Thanks."

"It's just the truth. I think this plan predates your cupcake topper." He sighed. "I wish we knew more about the connection between the two murders."

"When will we know for sure if the two are linked?" Though not much doubt remained in my mind, or Bastian's it seemed, at this point.

"I'm not sure. Seattle has a solid team but they move slowly, and they're not sharing information as well as I might hope. We have to work on the assumption that they are, because that's the most likely scenario."

I nodded, because my intuition—or at least my

common sense—agreed. "I don't suppose there's solid evidence in Cammi's murder pointing to a specific suspect...?"

"Not that Seattle's sharing."

"That's unfortunate."

"Hmm."

"Seattle wouldn't have recruited me to help, would they?"

"No." His reply came without hesitation.

"Thank you."

His gaze lifted to meet mine. "For extorting your help?"

"For letting me at least try to make this right."

He took a deep breath. "I didn't want to charge you. Not if I could find any way to avoid it. Your cooperation simply gives me a reasonable way to avoid it."

"Thank goodness. Witch prison doesn't sound like a spa trip."

He shot me a grim look. "No, no spa trip. On a related note, you do need to have a conversation with your family's mentor. Perhaps your great-aunt Sophia holds that role. You should call her and find out. I'd like to keep you out of prison, and learning the rules would be a helpful start."

"Sophia has known me my whole life. If she's the Dorchesters' mentor, then wouldn't she have seen my magic and known to get cracking with all the education?"

"You could have been a late bloomer. It's not unheard of."

"Hmm. If magic is on the Dorchester side of the family, I only have one cousin on that side. I could probably give him a poke and see if he happens to know anything. Discreetly, of course."

I had a feeling, whether it was intuition or complete guesswork, that the Clutterbucks (my mom's side of the family) weren't hiding any secret magical abilities.

I sent Bryson a quick text while I was thinking about it: *How do you feel about witches?*

Okay, so it wasn't subtle or discreet. But I didn't exactly out myself. I owned a Halloween-themed candy shop. I could be texting him about work.

He was probably in practice or working out and wouldn't get it till later, so I'd have to wait to see which way this conversation would go.

Except he wasn't in practice. His reply was immediate: *Trick question, right?*

No.

Before I could explain, a certain gorgeous widow, one whose life might be in danger, made an entrance through the coffee shop front door.

She swept in, paused, let the lesser humans gathered around her admire her beauty, then strutted to Bastian's and my corner.

I might be exaggerating...but only slightly.

My phone pinged with a text. I knew what waited —questions from my favorite cousin that I didn't have time to answer now that Delilah had arrived— so I stashed my phone.

"I demand protection." Delilah placed a well-manicured hand on her cocked hip. "You're the law around here. Make it happen."

In my peripheral vision, I caught a regular shaking her head at Delilah's dramatics. Which then had me looking around. No one seemed surprised.

I'd meant to ask when Hector had gone nuclear in front of Bastian's customers earlier today, but then I'd been sidetracked and had forgotten. Leaning closer to Bastian, I popped the pressing question. "Are only witches and wizards welcome here?"

In a normal tone of voice, Bastian replied, "No, we welcome everyone."

Delilah rolled her eyes, then gestured dismissively at the little people surrounding us—or so she implied. I rather liked the Magic Beans regulars. "They don't even know what we're talking about."

The young woman who'd shaken her head earlier snorted. "Everyone knows there's a murder investigation, Delilah. We're not idiots."

Wild guess: that particular regular was a witch.

Or wizard. Or if there were other magical people running around, then one of them.

Delilah turned so that her back was directly to the interloper. I made a note to introduce myself the next time we were both in Magic Beans and I wasn't unofficially contracted to find a killer.

"Protection, Bastian?"

"Certainly," Bastian replied. He didn't even look ruffled. He retrieved his phone from a pocket and started to scroll. "I'm sure Miles's brother can fit you into his schedule."

She paled. Literally, as I watched, her face lost color. "No. No, thank you."

Interesting. I added another item to my mental to-do list: definitely ask Miles about his brother.

"I'm not sure what you expect, then. I can't stop my investigation to be your personal protection detail."

And just like that, her attitude returned. "What investigation?" An accusatory stare followed her question.

Bastian and I might not have been discussing the case the very moment she walked in, but we were making progress.

Sort of.

And all evidence pointed to Bastian spending basically all of his time away from me digging into the case, researching, and reading Miles's research. I wasn't sure the man slept. Reading through all of Bitters's old wills alone would have taken him all night.

"Stop right there." I pointed a finger at her, but once I realized I had a rogue digit, I clasped my hands. Pointing was rude. "I know you've lost your husband and are grieving, and I'm sure you're scared with the killer still on the loose, but you can't expect such a small branch of the..." I stopped myself before I uttered the words International Criminal Witch Police. We were basically in public. "Such a small group of investigators to have the resources to solve a serious crime while simultaneously acting as your personal bodyguard."

When she arched a delicate eyebrow at Bastian, clearly expecting him to have some response, he said nothing. There was, however, an amused glint in his eyes.

Which just encouraged me. "And didn't you just inherit an obscene amount of money? Can't you hire someone?"

That comment didn't please her one bit. She wasn't wrong to be annoyed. It was crass to mention the money, but these were unique times. We were in the middle of a *murder* investigation.

"Ah, that, dear Lina, is the problem," Bastian said. "Milo Fortescue, Miles's brother, is the only game in town, and he has a certain reputation."

Turning to Delilah, he said, "I believe you've had dealings with Milo in the past?"

She narrowed her eyes. "You know I have."

In a whisper that she could clearly hear, he said, "Milo and Delilah used to date." But then he turned serious. "Hire him. Put the past aside."

She glared at him.

"Which is more important to you? Your pride or your safety?"

The gorgeous redhead chewed delicately on her lip. The action was at odds with her image of complete competence and control. She oozed confidence...but for the nibbling. After several seconds, she lifted her chin. "Fine. I'll pay the bill, but you're hiring him."

I didn't really understand what difference that made until Bastian pulled out his phone and made the call.

She really, really didn't want to speak to this Milo character. If he was anything like Miles, I couldn't understand it.

He was nothing like Miles.

Milo collected his new charge a mere ten minutes after the call was placed. Either his business was close to Magic Beans or he'd broken a number of speed limits.

When he walked in the door, I wondered for a brief moment if Magic Beans catered to giants. And this from a woman whose cousin played pro hockey. Bryson was a big guy, and all his college buddies and now colleagues were also big guys.

But they weren't Milo big. Or maybe it was the difference in attitude. Hockey players didn't look like they'd rip your arm off and snack on it if you made a wrong move.

Once they'd left, I said, "She'll be okay with him, right?"

Bastian laughed. "He's a puppy dog—unless you're a bad guy."

"So he's not a puppy dog, and I should be glad he's on our side."

Bastian shrugged.

That wasn't troubling. Not at all. But from what I'd learned of Delilah, she could hold her own.

"And what's with the Milo and Miles names?" I asked. "There's no way they're twins."

"No, Milo is older. And you'd have to ask his parents, but I can say that no one ever confuses the two of them." He picked up my empty coffee mug along with his own, then tipped his head at the office door. "Now that we have one less worry, let's track down Melanie."

10

W hy was my brother here?" Miles asked from behind Bastian's desk.

He didn't look up from the laptop screen or seem overly concerned, just curious.

"Picking up Delilah," Bastian replied. "He's on guard duty until we catch the killer."

He took the chair intended for guests, the one on the opposite side of the wide expanse of his desk.

His typically tidy space was covered in haphazard piles of paper. The mess made my skin itch, but Bastian—who I knew was scrupulously tidy —ignored the paper war zone.

"That's good," Miles replied in a distracted tone.

"Miles?" Bastian waited for his head barista, head researcher, and transport expert to lift his head from the laptop he was staring at intently.

That didn't happen.

"Miles, look at me."

Finally, Miles looked up. "You want her address."

"That's what I need."

"I found the agency Melanie used to book her weekend getaway, cross-referenced her recent gas purchase to narrow the potential properties, then looked at booking availability. Then I—"

"The address?" Bastian's patience was admirable. I wanted to shake Miles until his teeth rattled.

"I have something better." Miles grinned. "Unless you'd prefer to drive two hours over making a phone call."

"We've tried her number. She's not answering." Bastian crossed his arms.

Worse, her phone was switched off or set to do-not-disturb, because it rolled immediately to voicemail.

"I've got the boyfriend's name, his phone number, and the number for the cabin where I'm about eighty percent certain they're staying." He scrawled on a piece of notepaper as he spoke.

Bastian smiled and held out his hand. "Well done."

Miles smacked the scrap of paper onto Bastian's waiting palm. "I'll take a candy reward, thank you very much."

"Holland mints?" I asked, remembering one of his favorites.

"If those numbers pan out, then yes, please." He rubbed his eyes and covered a yawn. "Unless you have some other pressing need, I've got to get a few hours of sleep."

"How are you doing on Cammi and Rachael's files?" Bastian asked.

"I'm still working on them. Should be done tomorrow, but only if I can get some decent sleep." Miles frowned. "You know Rachael died in an accident that looked suspiciously not like an accident?"

"Can I revoke my witch card?" I asked. "It doesn't appear to be the safest occupation."

"It's not an occupation. It's who you are." Bastian pinned Miles with a probing look. "Explain."

"Accidental death was the official ruling, but the file was thin. Really thin." Miles rubbed his eyes again and sighed. Someone was coming down off his caffeine and sugar rush of earlier. "The file is older, and you know what it was like before you took over as the regional rep."

Bastian's reply was somewhere between a hum of agreement and a grunt. Boise's witch police must not have been stellar back... "When was this?" I asked.

"Late nineties," Bastian replied. "There wasn't much interest in pursuing anything but the most obvious and egregious of crimes."

"Are you saying, Miles, that you think Rachael Bitters, Bartholomew Bitters's first wife, might have been murdered over twenty years ago?" My mind was spinning with the possibilities. That certainly limited our suspect pool, if it was true and the murders were all connected.

"Maybe? I don't know. I need to beef up the case file, if I can. It's been so long…" He yawned again, his jaw cracking with the effort. "I'm just not sure I buy that her death was an accident."

"Get out of here. Get some sleep." Bastian indicated the door with a tip of his head. "We'll follow up with you after you've had some rest. Actually, why don't you let us know when you've got something."

"Will do, boss. And thanks for the desk and the laptop—but it'll be good to get back to my own tech." He frowned. "No touching the paperwork. I have a system."

Bastian didn't look happy. It seemed his comfort with the mess had been temporary.

"Just until I get the background files finished." Miles grinned. "You know you love my chaos…or at least my results."

"Yeah."

Miles must have taken Bastian's reply as an agreement to leave his chaotic system intact, because he was out the door in a flash.

Bastian looked down at the note still clutched in his hand and made an indecipherable noise.

"What does that mean?"

"I know Melanie's boyfriend. He's a wizard." He paused. "That's not typical."

"What?"

He pinned me with his gorgeous blue eyes. "Witches and wizards don't usually mix socially. Romantically."

And that answered the question that had been bouncing around in my head earlier. I must have had an idea, on some level, that Bastian felt that way. Why else would I draw a distinction in my mind between witches and wizards? I was new to magic. Magic people were magic people, as far I knew.

Now he was telling me... Not that it was forbidden. What was he telling me? "Why don't they mix?"

He took a breath, opened his mouth—then paused. "I need to call Callum." He lifted the note.

He really did know this Callum guy. He didn't even have to punch in the phone number on his cell; Callum was programmed in his contacts.

The status of witch-wizard relations would have to be dissected another time. I wasn't letting go of that particular topic...because I needed a better understanding of my new community. No other reason.

Bastian and Callum discussed Melanie's safety and keeping her out of Boise.

It was a brief conversation, over in two or three minutes. Very calm, very efficient. And though I couldn't hear Callum's end of the conversation, it had been clear the other man hadn't responded in an overtly emotional way.

"Keeping a level head in a crisis, is that a wizard characteristic or just one you and your friends share?" I asked.

"Callum's not my friend."

"He's programmed in your phone."

"He's an acquaintance." Bastian turned in his chair to fully face me. I'd chosen my favorite seat, the couch. "And to answer your question, wizards do have a reputation for being level-headed. Remember, that's where our magic comes from. If a wizard lets emotions rule, then his magic suffers."

So strange. And at some point, that strangeness would have to be addressed. I'd have to fill in my educational gaps.

Education reminded me that I needed to figure out who played the role of mentor in my family. And once I was thinking of family...Bryson! I snatched my phone from my pocket.

I had several missed texts from my cousin, each escalating in concern over my simple inquiry about witches. The second to last read, "Call me," and the last told me he had to grab a nap before his game this evening, but that we needed to talk.

"Everything all right?" Bastian asked.

"Yes, I just... I think maybe Bryson knows more about our family's connection to magic than I do." I looked up at Bastian. I was confused, maybe hurt. No, definitely hurt. "I don't have any siblings, and Bryson is my closest cousin. Not in age, but we've always been friends."

"This is your cousin who plays professional hockey?"

"Yeah. He's playing for the American Hockey League right now, but he's hoping to get called up to the NHL." I shook my head, because that had nothing to do with anything.

So he was ten years younger than me, and he had a busy life filled with skating and weightlifting and who knew what all professional hockey players did—but we were still close, even these days. We texted. We saw each other...occasionally. When family events happened.

"Gosh, I guess it's been a while since I've seen him in person." I thought back. Maybe Great Aunt Sophia's husband's funeral? And that had been a little while ago.

Bastian leaned forward, resting his forearms on his thighs. "The code of conduct makes it clear that we're not to discuss magical matters with nonmagical people, even family members. So if Bryson inherited magic but didn't know that you had, he wouldn't have been able to speak with you about it."

"Hmm. Yeah, I suppose I understand that." I didn't. Not really. We were family. He was my favorite cousin. Almost like a brother. Heck, I didn't have a brother, so in my world he basically played that role.

Bastian's phone rang. "That will be Melanie. She was in the shower earlier. Callum said he'd have her call once he explained everything."

I nodded as he answered his phone and exchanged greetings with Melanie.

"I'm putting you on speaker." Bastian placed his phone on the corner of his desk atop a stack of paper and tapped it once. "Lina Dorchester is with me. She's a local witch aiding in the investigation."

"Hi, Lina. I'm glad Bastian has help. I know the Boise office is small." Melanie didn't sound at all like I'd expected her to. Or rather, like *I* would if I thought someone had me on their murder to-do list. She was calm.

"I'm sorry your weekend getaway has been interrupted by...unpleasantness."

She chuckled. "Unpleasantness? Is that what we're calling murder these days?" But then the line went quiet. When she spoke again her voice was more subdued. "Involving myself with Bartholomew Bitters was one of the biggest mistakes of my life, topped only by marrying him. I can't say I'm shocked that choice is still haunting me, but I'm disappointed."

"Callum says the two of you can stay indoors for the remainder of your visit?" Bastian indicated the chair he'd abandoned as he waited for Melanie to reply.

I shook my head and leaned against the edge of his desk.

"Not a problem." She chuckled again. "Callum and I can definitely entertain ourselves inside. And I've called the rental company. We've extended our stay. I have plenty of vacation, and in a pinch, I've got my laptop with me. If you think I'll be safer here, then I'll stay put."

Looked like this ex-wife had definitely moved on, given she'd all but said she and Callum would be rolling around naked in bed for the foreseeable future.

"Yes. We haven't definitively tied the murder in Seattle to our case, but we suspect they're connected. If they are, then we know the killer is willing to travel. But if you don't leave the house, stay with Callum so you've got an extra set of eyes, and remain vigilant, you should be fine. And eat in. Bitters was killed with an edible curse."

"No problem. We brought groceries, but I'll have Callum double-check all of our supplies." She cleared her throat. "I understand that you wanted to talk to me about Bartholomew?"

"Yes. We're trying to draw connections, discover who might be motivated to kill him and also Cammi."

"All right. Let's do this. What do you want to know?" Her tone was grim but determined.

"Who initiated the divorce?" Bastian didn't dance around.

"I did when I found out he was cheating on me."

"With Delilah?" I asked, for purposes of clarity.

"Actually, no, but good guess. He did cheat on Rachael with Cammi, but I believe that was the last of his wives to, ah, overlap. He certainly slept around on all of his wives. Except maybe Delilah. That I'm not sure about. But Rachael, Cammi, me—he wasn't faithful to any of us. He didn't even try to hide his affairs, not from us, just the court."

"He alleged that he'd been faithful during the divorce proceedings?" Bastian asked.

"He had to. He had to allege his own fidelity while bringing ours into question, otherwise he was required to pay a divorce settlement per the prenuptial agreements we all signed. Not a sizable settlement, but Bartholomew ever was one to scrimp where he could."

"What?" I snapped. "You're kidding me. He slept with other women, claimed fidelity, and then broke the prenuptial agreements he made with each of his exes by falsely accusing them of affairs?"

"Yes, he did. He was a gem like that." Melanie snorted. "Did I just move up the suspect list? Because, really, I was almost angry enough to murder the jerk for a good year or so. It wasn't the money or even the cheating in the end. It was all the lying. The false accusations. I might have been ready for the marriage to end, but I certainly never had an affair. Even if it's something I thought I could have lived with, I didn't have interest in men by that point. Not at the end of the marriage and not after. Not until Callum."

"We'll be sure to make a note of your motive," Bastian said.

I wanted to thump him, but Melanie laughed. "You wizards and your dry sense of humor. Good thing I'm dating one, or I might think you were serious." The teasing tone vanished as she added, "Find who did this, Bastian. He was a jerk, but I think... well, I think maybe he loved Delilah. Or as close as he could get to it. He was a miserably unhappy man when I knew him, and that had an effect on how he treated the people around him. He was miserable, he could be mean, but he was capable of change. And he certainly didn't deserve to be murdered."

I wanted to promise her we'd find justice for Bitters and for Cammi.

Bastian spoke first, however, with a much more realistic promise. "We'll do what we can to find the killer. Is there anything else that might help us? Anything from your time with him, any enemies that stand out?"

"Other than his terrible family? No. And, honestly, I doubt his family would be capable of any kind of murder plot. They'd be more likely to stab him with a steak knife at one of their dinner parties. They're more prone to in-the-heat-of-the-moment crimes."

I coughed to cover the unexpected bark of laughter her comment elicited.

"I see you've met the family, Lina." Her wry tone was unmistakable as she added, "Lovely, aren't they?"

"I've only met Hector in person, but yes, that was my impression. Planning and patience didn't seem to be his strengths."

She made a grumbling noise. "They give witches a bad name. Embracing a lack of discipline and calling it passion. The Bitters are not my kind of people, and I'm ashamed I ever allied myself with the family." She sighed. "Callum is fussing at me. If you don't have any more questions?"

"No," Bastian said. "But keep your phone turned on and charged. Both you and Callum, so we can get in touch quickly if there's a change."

"Of course, already done. Thank you. For tracking us down and keeping us informed. And good luck."

We both stared at the phone now.

I knew what I was thinking—that I believed Melanie, that I was happy she'd found her person, that everyone deserved a second chance in love, even Bitters but especially Melanie, and that I really didn't understand what Bastian had been going on about with his 'witches and wizards don't mingle' comment—but I was fairly certain Bastian's thoughts were headed in a different direction.

"Witches and wizards don't usually date," he said.

Or maybe he was a mind reader.

"Why not?"

"They're incompatible on a fundamental level."

"Humph." Oops. I hadn't meant to give voice to my exasperation. Then again, in for a penny... "That's garbage."

He quirked an eyebrow. "How do you know? You've known you're a witch for—" He glanced at his watch. "Around twenty-four hours now. And you know exactly one wizard."

Aww, wasn't he just adorable?

I grinned. "I know me, and I know you. And I know I'd date a man like you in a heartbeat."

Oops. I could think that sort of thing in my head, but saying it? No, saying it was a bad, bad idea.

Bastian and I worked together. On a murder investigation that we were in the middle of.

And my life, which had been on track and moving in a very specific direction, had taken a hard left into the unknown.

I turned on my heel and headed for the bathroom. Because I had to powder my nose right now. This very second.

That's why I hoofed it out of Bastian's office at lightning speed. Two cups of coffee and a full bladder were why.

Not because I'd spoken words aloud that couldn't be taken back.

Words I should regret but couldn't.

Words I couldn't act on, much as I might like to.

11

The problem with making bold statements and then running away like a teenage boy who's passed gas at the dinner table during a first date?

Just like that flatulent teen, you have to go back.

But not right away.

I washed my hands, dried them thoroughly, checked my teeth, considered other stalling tactics, and finally landed on ordering a drink.

I'd never actually made it to the counter at Magic Beans to order.

Drinks always appeared, having been intuited by a staff member with a "feel" for coffee, or were ordered from passing staff as they bussed tables.

As I approached the counter, I realized I didn't have my purse. But Hanna was working, and she was one of the witchy crowd. Actually, I was fairly certain that while customers might be a mix of magical and nonmagical, all of the staff were of the witch variety.

Hanna smiled. She seemed more comfortable in her skin than earlier. Maybe she was getting into the rhythm of working at Magic Beans.

Although she still didn't make eye contact. I'd bet she could describe my left earlobe in precise detail.

"You're settling in?" I asked.

She rolled her lips together, then nodded.

If I was reading her body language correctly—and I was no slouch in that department—she'd just bitten back a comment.

"Is everything okay?"

She tilted her head. "Why do you ask?" She looked around the almost empty store, as if searching for a flaw. As if I'd spotted some failure on her part.

But the seating area had been bussed and wiped down, the trash wasn't yet ready to go out, and the few lingering customers appeared relaxed and happy. I couldn't even imagine why she'd think I was being critical.

I flashed a friendly smile, trying to reassure her. "No reason. You make fantastic coffee drinks. Magic Beans is lucky to have you."

She smiled, again, not quite meeting my gaze. She really was terribly shy. "Maybe an Italian soda?"

I hadn't actually been craving a drink, just

looking for a way to delay returning to the office, but that sounded perfect. I was about to tell her light on the syrup but stopped myself and nodded.

Giving instructions to someone who created the perfect drink every time was insulting, and I didn't want Hanna to think I didn't value her skills or trust her judgment.

When she handed me the drink—Italian soda, light raspberry syrup—she said, "Everything's going well with the investigation?"

Bastian and I hadn't made time to discuss the ins and outs of investigative protocols. For example, how secretive was our investigation? And did all Magic Beans staff know how the case was progressing, or just Miles and Sabrina?

Apparently, I dithered too long, because Hanna said, "Sorry! It's just that Miles has been so busy since he hired me, and I know you're all working on the murder case."

"Cases. There are two." Which we actually were only guessing at this point, so I added, "Maybe. But you know Miles; he's a research whiz. He'll untangle any connections between the two cases—if there are any."

She nodded, but I'd lost her attention to the customer who'd snuck in behind me and was waiting patiently to order.

Time to face the music.

Except...there was no music.

Bastian looked up from the armchair where he'd planted himself with his laptop. His attempt to escape the chaos of his desk—or just trying to keep Miles's piles of paperwork intact. "I've been reviewing the players, using your murder board and the Bitters family email group membership list."

If he didn't want to talk about my embarrassing comment, that was fine by me. "Do you think we're missing an important area of his life? We've focused on his ex-wives and his family, but was he involved in any business ventures? If this is how he treats the people in his personal life..."

"Actually, I've done business with him. His personal life may be a mess and full of questionable ethical decisions—"

I snorted.

"All right. It was full of worse-than-questionable ethical decisions," Bastian corrected himself. "But his reputation in the business world is squeaky clean."

"That's odd."

"Is it? Many people have contextual values."

I squinted at him, not sure I was understanding. "How do you mean?"

"Many people believe that killing a person if you're protecting yourself is morally acceptable, but that death for financial gain is not, for example."

I blinked. I still didn't follow.

He sighed. "Consider what Melanie said about Bitters's state of mind. He may have felt justified in his actions against his former wives, which would have made the breaking of those contracts by any means possible an ethical choice in his mind."

"Don't tell me you think what he did was acceptable."

He looked surprised. "Of course not. I'm merely giving one possible explanation for the apparent inconsistency between how he handled business contracts versus legal agreements with the women in his life."

"Hmm. Or he was a misogynist." When Bastian arched an eyebrow but refused to address my comment, I said, "Fine. I have no proof of that. I do know he treated the women in his *personal* life appallingly."

"Yes, there's ample evidence of that. But back to your point, I think this murder is personal. I don't think someone has reached out to harm him after a business deal gone wrong."

"Why?" I swallowed a smile. Was Bastian relying on intuition? Or was he merely synthesizing all of the information he'd thus far collected?

"As I said before, he has a long history of ethical professional interactions, and yet, there's an abundance of evidence that he manipulated his family with promises of future wealth, was unfaithful to the women in his life, and generally treated his wives with an appalling lack of respect."

"Fair enough. Any chance he'd have involved Cammi in his business?"

"From what I know of him personally and what I've learned over the last few days? Doubtful. He didn't mix his business and personal lives." Bastian snapped his laptop shut, stood, and stretched.

I didn't ogle him. Not the pleasant bulge of his biceps under his T-shirt sleeves, nor the small strip of revealed skin just above the waistband of those terrible cargo pants.

When he was done, I quickly averted my eyes. Not that I'd been ogling.

"I need a coffee." He frowned and looked at the door.

At which point I realized how unusual that sentiment was. The staff at Magic Beans had a preternatural skill for anticipating orders. Part and parcel with that "feel" for coffee Miles and Bastian so eagerly sought in their employees, I supposed.

As I pondered the oddness of having to actually go to the counter and order—and not as a delaying tactic—a knock sounded on the door.

"Enter," Bastian called.

A redhead with a broad, easy smile poked her

head in. "Heya, boss. Bet you didn't think you'd see me again."

"Hi, Bethann." He gave her a quizzical look, which I was sure I shared. She'd quit, last I heard.

"Miles begged me to come back until either another staff person could be hired or Sabrina's loan to Sticky Tricky Treats ended. I told him yes, but only if he didn't complain when I waited for customers to order and didn't try to second-guess every request." For someone who couldn't run away from this job fast enough just a day ago, she seemed surprisingly chipper to be here again. "Can I get either of you anything?"

"We're glad to have you fill in," Bastian replied, and then proceeded to actually order his own coffee. A black dark roast pour-over.

When she turned to me, I pointed to my half full Italian soda. "I'm good. I grabbed a drink from Hanna a few minutes ago."

"Oh, yeah. Sorry, boss. That's why I'm taking your order. When I got here about five minutes ago, Hanna headed out early. She said she had a family emergency. I told her it was no problem. Hope that's okay. I'll just stay to close if you can't get a regular staffer back in."

He shook his head. "No need, if you're comfortable here by yourself."

She grinned. "Absolutely. It's all the coffee magic

hoo-ha that stressed me out. If I can just fill orders and take money, I'm tickled to be here—even if it's temporary."

Once the door clicked shut behind her smiling face, I turned to Bastian with a critical look.

He lifted his hands defensively. "We didn't fire her. She quit."

"Because you people have unreasonable expectations with all your talk of having a 'feel' for coffee." I thought of Lucy, my more-than-adequate shop help. If I'd waited to find an employee with a "feel" for candy, I wouldn't have found her and she was a gem in so many ways.

Bastian wandered over to his desk and scanned the top layer of paperwork.

"I bet your pour-over is great." Just because Bethann didn't have the "feel" didn't mean she made bad coffee.

He started to flip through a pile near the corner of his desk, changed his mind, and then turned to a file cabinet in the corner of the office. He pulled out a key ring with around half a dozen keys from one of his many pockets and then unlocked the cabinet.

He stopped suddenly and turned to me. "I'm sorry. What were you saying?"

"Just that I'd bet Bethann makes a mean dark roast pour-over."

"I won't take that bet. She makes an exceptional

cup of coffee. She just doesn't have the feel, and when you work side by side with Miles and Sabrina, it's hard not to feel inadequate. Also, it makes our customers feel special when you can anticipate their needs—and remember their order after you've had the same drink a time or two."

"Oh, good point. You do always get the same drink, don't you?" But Bastian wasn't listening. His attention was once again on his task as he flipped through file folders.

I walked close enough to see he'd pulled a personnel file. "What in the world are you doing?"

He didn't look up from the file he was reading. "Call Miles." He pulled his phone out of a pocket and started to enter a number from the file folder. He glanced at me just long enough to see I'd gotten my phone out and then rattled off Miles's number.

I tapped CALL and waited. The phone rang and rang. Miles didn't pick up and eventually an electronic voice informed me that Miles had failed to set up his mailbox. "You have got to be kidding me."

"No, that's fine. Apologies for the disturbance." Bastian ended the call and turned to me. I couldn't read the expression on his face.

"Miles didn't pick up. I didn't leave a voicemail, because—"

"No, I know. Text him that I want to talk to him

as soon as possible. I'm sure he's passed out and didn't hear his phone."

That made sense, given how tired he'd been when he left. Research for this case had him keeping odd hours, so it wasn't any great surprise.

I noticed that Bastian had pulled a page from the file and was referencing it as he tapped on his phone.

I sent Miles a quick message telling him to call Bastian as soon as he woke up.

"Yes, thank you for your time." He ended the call and dialed again. "Hello, this is Bastian Heissman, owner of Magic Beans coffee shop. I'm calling regarding a reference for Hanna Sellers." He caught my glance, and I shivered at the look there. But then he blinked, and his focus was again on the phone call. "Yes, that's correct. I'm calling to verify employment."

Hanna? Why was he calling around about Hanna? And wouldn't that have been done when she was hired?

He retrieved a pen and notepad from one of the drawers and scribbled as the person on the phone continued to speak. "Thank you. And I appreciate you sharing that information."

When he ended the call, I said, "What in the world are you—"

He held up a hand as he entered the number

he'd scratched out earlier. "Hello, this is Bastian Heissman." And he repeated the same information as before, explaining who he was and why he was calling. When he ended the third call, there was no doubt that his expression was grim.

"What's going on with Hanna?" I asked.

"Have you ever made eye contact with her?"

"What?" But I knew what—I just didn't understand *why* he was asking the question. I thought back to the few interactions I'd had with her, and then I scrunched up my nose. "She always looks at my left earlobe. I thought it was odd, but she's also shy, so it's not *that* odd."

"I don't think she's shy."

"Bastian, what's going on?"

"You're a new witch, so it's possible you wouldn't be able to spot someone who'd used your magic recently...but I think you might."

"And I'd spot it when I made eye contact with this person?"

He was only half listening to me, because he was dialing once again. After waiting several rings with no response, he ended the call and then immediately began to type a message in his phone.

When he was done, he looked up. "Yes, it's in the eyes."

"That would have been nice to know." I collapsed into the sofa and squeezed my eyes shut as I considered how many suspects I'd met and made eye contact with. "Preferably before I met a dozen murder suspects."

He frowned at me. "Not a dozen."

I frowned back. "Close enough."

He started to flip through Miles's papers. Good thing he didn't argue the point, because anything beyond one person when it came to meeting people who might have murdered another human being was too many, especially when I was a possible liability to him or her. He wasn't going to win that particular argument.

"It's not always visible. There are tricks to hide it. And I didn't want to trigger any false positives. Or to worry you." He looked up from his deep dive into the chaos on his desk. "You weren't in any danger."

I told him with one look just how much I thought of that particular assertion.

"All right." He looked annoyed. "You weren't in any more danger than you would have been had you continued to run your shop oblivious of your newly unleashed magic."

"How do you know that?"

"Because you've been with Miles, Sabrina, or me ever since I recruited you, or at home, in your car, or in your shop where I have protections in place."

I blinked. "What did you do to my shop? My car? And my house?"

"I did my best to keep you safe, while you put off having any conversations with your family's mentor and came to terms with being a witch." He was still flipping through Miles's paperwork, but he looked up at me in between scanning pages.

"Oh." It had only been a day—a day and a half if I was persnickety—since I'd learned about witches and warlocks and wizards. And even if I was genetically preprogrammed to believe in magic, like Miles had explained, it was...a lot. "You were giving me time."

"Yes."

I was about to express my thanks—because I did need time, and I appreciated Bastian trying to give me that space to process—but then a thought popped into my head. Not a thought, a worry. A worrisome thought.

"Does Miles usually sleep through phone calls?"

"Depends on whether he's silenced his phone or not, and that's a function of how tired he is and how much he thinks he needs to sleep in order to work efficiently."

"When I ordered my drink from Hanna earlier, I mentioned Miles and the Seattle murder. I said that he was a research whiz and he'd untangle any connections between them. And now you seem to think Hanna—"

He stopped shuffling papers and headed straight

for the exterior exit. But then he paused with his hand on the doorknob, muttered a few incomprehensible words, then turned back to me. "You should wait here. In the office."

His office, which not everyone could open. Which obviously had mysterious protections that I could neither see nor feel. An office which I'd bet Hanna could no longer enter.

He was trying to keep me safe...which meant he anticipated trouble for Miles.

"No." I pushed him out the door. "And you don't have time to argue with me."

He didn't. Because I'd sent a potential killer after the person digging up all her secrets.

12

Once Bastian and I were in the car and headed to Miles's apartment, I asked, "How certain are you that Hanna's the murderer?"

"Bethann said Hanna had a family emergency. Hanna doesn't have any family. When she listed her roommate as her emergency contact on her employment paperwork, I asked."

Bastian was worried. There was no mirror-checking. None. And he was speeding.

"What did her references say? I assume that's who you were calling, her previous employers from her résumé."

"Yes, and she didn't lie about her work history." His hands gripped the steering wheel tightly.

"But...?"

"But references have difficulty concealing red

flags. If there's something off about their former colleague, you can tell. Even if it's only the waver in the human resources manager's voice when they confirm dates of employment."

"And there was a waver?"

"There was a waver. And I also caught a concerned employee who gave me the number of another employer she suspected Hanna might not have listed on her résumé."

"And what did that employer say?"

"Nothing definitive, but the woman who answered the phone expressed concern for Hanna. She asked if she was doing better now."

I blinked, because... "Well, that could mean anything."

"Why lie about a family emergency? Why won't she make eye contact with you? Add in Miles not answering his phone, and her troubling references, and, yes, I'm worried." He tapped his thumb on the steering wheel. The tempo was much faster than usual, and he didn't make it to ten. "And one of the piles on my desk had to do with a child. Rachael's child."

"Wait, what? Bitters had a child with his first wife?" That couldn't be right. There was no mention of her on social media. "Was she included in the family group email distribution?"

"No."

"And you would have mentioned if she'd been included in a will."

Bastian nodded his head. "I wasn't aware Bitters had a child."

And Bastian actually knew Bartholomew Bitters. "You should have known, right?"

"Yes. The magical tend to mix with the magical, and everyone knows everyone else's business. I would expect to know if he had a daughter."

"Maybe Hanna isn't Bitters's child?" I spun through a few different scenarios. "Say she cheated on him. That might explain his attitude toward women."

Bastian frowned at me, which made me evaluate what I'd said.

"Right. That is a massive leap, and completely unfair to the deceased woman." I looked skyward and murmured an apology. "But we don't even know if Hanna is this child that Miles discovered."

"We don't."

I sighed. "But it fits."

Bastian pulled into a small apartment complex. There couldn't have been more than twenty units. It wasn't at all what I would have expected. I would have put Miles in a downtown apartment in some colorful and fun part of Boise. This was nice, just unexpected.

It was close to Magic Beans, though. It probably

took him about the same amount of time to walk to work as it did to drive.

As Bastian put the Crosstrek in park, he said, "You should stay in the car."

"Uh-uh. That's not happening." Then common sense asserted itself. "But you can go first."

He was the one with all the skill and training, after all. Oh, and also the actual law enforcement officer.

With a final grim look my direction, he hopped out of the car and jogged through the parking lot and up a set of stairs.

Unlike Miles, I did actually exercise, so I sprinted after him and caught up before he made it to Miles's door. A purple door. Which was when I noticed that each of the doors was painted a different color. Some bright, some bold, none boring. Maybe this place suited Miles more than I'd initially thought.

Bastian wrapped his hand around my wrist and pulled me to a stop about two feet from the door. I felt a warmth pulse through me, originating from his hand.

I yanked my arm away and whisper-yelled, "Did you just magic me?"

Bastian closed his eyes and shook his head, except it wasn't a denial. More an exasperated gesture. With a look that clearly said, "Remember that promise you made?" he stepped in front of me.

I couldn't even see the door from behind his broad back, but I could tell he reached out and did something to it.

The lock clicked and the door swung quietly open. Someone had been oiling their hinges.

Bastian extended his hand in the classic "wait" gesture, and then stepped across the threshold. Two heartbeats later, I let out a breath I didn't know I was holding as Bastian's rigid posture relaxed.

"She's not here," he said over his shoulder before walking further into the apartment. "Miles?"

I scanned the apartment and found it shockingly tidy for a man whose organizational system for research involved haphazard stacks of paper.

His kitchen was immaculate, his living room almost barren. I followed Bastian down a hallway with three doors. Behind the first was a bedroom currently functioning as an office, where I finally saw some evidence of Miles's trademark organized mess.

For a twenty-something, he sure did like his paper. He even had a fancy printer set up in the corner on its very own table.

Before I could do more than note the existence of the papers tacked to the wall alongside several whiteboards, Bastian had moved on.

The bathroom appeared to be pristine. Perhaps

it was an unused guest bath, or Miles was a better housekeeper than I'd ever have guessed.

The final door revealed a bedroom.

And Miles.

"Why is he still sleeping?" Horror struck as I searched for a telltale lifting of his chest. And his face seemed quite pale—or was that the lighting? "He is sleeping, isn't he?"

Only when Bastian squeezed my fingers reassuringly did I realize I'd grabbed his hand. "He's asleep, it's just not a natural sleep."

The relief I felt when he confirmed that Miles hadn't been killed faded when the full meaning of his words registered. "He's been magicked? What did she do to him? Can you fix it? Oh my gosh, this is all my fault."

"Promise you won't slap me."

"What?" I lifted panicked, guilt-ridden eyes to Bastian's. What was he talking about?

"You need to calm down."

And then I laughed. It was a little bit because Bastian knew enough about women to know that telling one to calm down wasn't the smartest thing to say. And it was a little because I was beginning to recognize his dry sort of humor.

If Bastian could crack a joke, however small, then Miles was going to be fine.

There might also have been a touch of hysteria

in my laughter, but I'd deny it later. I wasn't a hysterical sort of woman. Or I hadn't been, before I'd discovered I was a witch.

"He's going to be okay?"

"Yes, but I can't wake him up if I'm worried about you."

I blinked at him, confused. And then it occurred to me exactly what he was saying.

Bastian needed to tap into his logical self to work magic. He needed to be cool as a cucumber to do whatever needed doing to wake up Miles.

"No offense, but witch magic has your wizarding variety beat, hands down. If y'all can't work magic in the midst of a crisis, what good is it having magic at all?"

He gave me a funny look as he knelt by Miles. "It's not usually a problem."

With one knee on the ground, he touched three fingers to Miles's temple. He'd done exactly the same to me when he'd healed my headache.

This time, though, it wasn't a simple touch and done.

Bastian closed his eyes and muttered something —I couldn't hear what—over and over again. I finally realized that he was mouthing the words, making no sound at all.

Maybe it was a prayer. Maybe an incantation. I

didn't know how to use my own magic, let alone how wizard magic was invoked, so I was only guessing.

As soon as everything calmed down—when we had the murderer firmly identified and under wraps and I'd reclaimed the shop keys currently in Sabrina's possession—then I'd make the dreaded call that would begin my witchy education, the one to Great Aunt Sophia.

Which reminded me that I needed to make an even more difficult one to Bryson. I knew I'd have to forgive him, that there wasn't really anything to forgive, but I was still mad as heck at him right now.

Bastian's silent words came to a halt and his eyes opened.

But Miles's didn't.

That couldn't be good. But maybe he just needed a nudge. "Miles?" I called out, a little louder than was strictly necessary if he'd been sleeping the sleep of a normal person who hadn't been enchanted by a pissed-off, murdering witch.

He didn't stir, and Bastian sighed. Then he turned to me.

Except he didn't say anything.

"What's wrong?"

"I need your help." His voice was even. Calm.

But I could tell that he was worried. "What aren't you saying?" And why would he need *my* help? I was the untrained newbie who hadn't done any magic outside of some accidental cursing.

And then it hit me. About twenty seconds after a normal person, one who wasn't stuck in the land of denial.

"Oh, no, *she did not.*" That evil, conniving witch had used my cursed cupcake topper to knock Miles into an unnatural sleep.

"Yeah, she did."

"But she only had the one." It had been a simple matter of inventory. Only one cupcake topper had been sold. Bastian had confiscated the rest.

"Then she didn't use all of the original to curse Bitters."

"Please tell me this isn't what she did to Bitters. Please." Miles was sweet. He was helpful, hardworking, a little awkward, but eager and good-hearted. He couldn't be—

"Hey, Lina. Listen to me." At which point I realized that I hadn't been listening to him. I'd been falling into a deep, dark pit of blame.

"Sorry," I whispered.

"I was saying that he'll be fine. Even if we can't reverse it, he'll wake up...eventually."

"Eventually?" I practically shrieked. I couldn't resist checking to see if my hollering had woken our sleeping friend, but no such luck.

"Yes, eventually. I don't know when, but I do

know this wasn't intended to be lethal. Whoever did this—" He looked really mad. Really, unwizardly, un-Bastian-like mad.— "Probably Hanna, but until we have proof, *whoever* did this, they didn't mean to kill him, just keep him out of the way for a little while."

"Oh." The implication hit me like a ton of bricks. "Oh, no, Bastian. That means that she has someone else on her hit list."

"Or at least some kind of unfinished business. But, yes, I suspect she has another victim in her sights. Miles must have information regarding the identity of her next victim, hence needing him out of the way temporarily." Bastian looked at me. "Can you help me wake him up?"

I nodded until I felt like a bobblehead, because yes, so many times yes. "I'll do whatever you tell me."

13

M ental note: before promising someone that I'd do "whatever they told me," consider *not* making that promise.

That was the promise of a frantic, desperate woman who wasn't thinking clearly.

"You can do this." Bastian handed me a small paring knife he'd retrieved from Miles's kitchen. It was comforting, for some reason, that he hadn't had that particular item stashed in one of his many pockets. Cuffs, yes. Knives, no.

"Right." I *could* do this...I just didn't *want* to.

"It's a tiny cut." Bastian was trying to reassure me, but so long as there was a knife in my hand and an expectation I use it on human flesh, I wasn't going to be reassured.

"Are you sure I can't just use my blood?" I glared at him. "Or yours?"

My conscience wasn't loving Bastian's brilliant idea to slice and dice a sleeping man. Warning bells were ringing, telling me this was wrong, and wasn't I supposed to listen closely to my intuition?

"It's not about the blood. It's about the cutting."

Right. I knew that. He'd already explained it to me. Bastian's grand plan was for me to "focus and cut." Something about the cutting of Miles's skin would "cut" the spell away from him.

I'd just been hyperfocused on the blood, because...blood.

"A small cut. I can do this." I moved the knife closer to Miles, then stopped. He was completely unaware of what was happening around him. Utterly defenseless. "Explain to me again why this is the only option?"

"Because you don't yet understand your own magic. Because you also don't have the focus necessary to work magic. Because cutting the spell away from him without a parallel physical act is beyond your capabilities."

"And you can't do it."

His finger tapped a rapid-fire tattoo against his thigh. "I've already tried."

Except I hadn't seen *him* slicing Miles in his attempt to cut the spell away from his friend. Ugh. If

I didn't hurry up and do this, then the killer would get that much more of a head start.

I picked up Miles's arm, lifted the knife, and thought about what I was going to do. I got a good picture in my head, because I didn't want to make this any worse than it already was.

Quick, neat, shallow.

A single swipe and I'd cut away the magic holding him in an unnatural slumber.

One swipe with the tip of the blade.

Quick, neat, shallow.

Cutting away the foreign magic clinging to him.

I inhaled and held my breath, thinking, "Quick, neat, shallow."

Miles's arm jerked away from my hand. "What the ever-loving—"

"Miles!" I screeched his name. All the last several minutes' tension released in one shouted word. I lifted my hand to my rapidly beating heart, except there was still a knife in it. I stashed it on his nightstand.

"Why are you both in my room?" Propped up on his elbows, he glared at the knife and then me. "And why did it look like you were about to open up one of my veins?"

"I was cutting away the sleep spell that Hanna —was it Hanna?—anyway, I was cutting away the spell that *someone* put on you." Poor guy. He was probably disoriented from all that magic napping.

"I'm sorry—you what?" He sat up and turned so that his feet were planted firmly on the floor. Then he glared—at me, at Bastian, at his arm.

That was when I noticed that he didn't seem groggy at all, and he was still looking at me like I was a mass murderer. Or maybe like I was a vampire ready to suck all the blood from his body. Either way, not fondly, and certainly not as if I had broken an evil spell holding him in an unnatural slumber.

Apparently, slicing up sleeping-spelled people wasn't standard operating procedure.

My almost-victim was mad, I was confused, and only one person here knew what was going on. So I did what any mature woman in a similar situation would do. Pointing a finger at Bastian, I said, "He made me do it."

"Out of bed." Bastian motioned with his hand, as if that would hurry Miles onto his feet. "We need you awake and sharp. We have questions only you can answer."

Miles's rear remained planted on his mattress, and he crossed his arms. "Not until you tell me why I was about to be attacked in my bed by a witch wielding my favorite paring knife."

"She hasn't had any training, and it seemed like a good analogy."

"She" was getting a clue that Bastian had perpetrated a rather large deceit upon her. Her, meaning me. "You lied."

Some of my appalled sensibilities must have shone through, because Miles patted my arm reassuringly. "He does that, but always for the greater good."

"But he told me to assault a defenseless man." I blinked. "With a knife."

"Can we please move past this?" Bastian ran a hand through his hair. Since that seemed a few steps beyond finger-tapping, I made myself listen before he lost all of his patience. "First, Lina, I apologize. It was a necessary deception, since I couldn't cut through the combination of your cursing magic and the sleep spell."

"Oh. She supercharged a sleeping spell with Lina's curse magic? Clever." Miles raised his eyebrows. "Also, thank you. Both of you. That could have had me sleeping through what's left of my twenties."

I snapped my mouth shut. Gaping wasn't helpful, and he was probably exaggerating for effect anyway.

"And second," Bastian raised his voice slightly, "you need to tell us who spelled you, Miles."

"Oh, I thought you already knew. Hanna." He rubbed the back of his neck. Then looked up at

Bastian with guilt plastered all over his face. "I didn't know, boss. I hired her, and I didn't know."

"None of us knew. We all met her, talked to her." Bastian raised his eyebrows. "Drank her coffee."

"Yeah. She really does make great coffee. She has the feel." Miles shook his head, if I wasn't mistaken, mourning the loss of yet another barista.

"Come on. Let's get some caffeine in you." Bastian clasped Miles's shoulder. "We think Hanna might have another victim and that you stumbled across information that points to that person."

"I don't stumble across information," Miles replied as he stood up. He swayed until Bastian placed a steadying hand on his arm. "I compile information from various sources, draw meaningful conclusions, and summarize them concisely for my boss, who doesn't like to read long reports."

Poor Miles. Attacked by his employee, almost assaulted in his sleep by a newbie witch, and now Bastian was giving him grief over his process. He really wasn't having a great day.

"I'm sure Bastian appreciates your reports," I said as I followed him into his kitchen.

When Bastian didn't reply, I poked him in the ribs. He grunted, then said, "Most days. But we need to shortcut the process this time."

"I get it, boss." When he tried to prep his own

coffee, I shoved him toward a seat at the kitchen table.

"Why don't you discuss possibilities while I make the coffee." They shared a look, which had me pointing at them. My mother would be very displeased by the development of this particular habit. "You two, shush. I can make coffee."

I puttered in Miles's kitchen, grinding beans, rooting in his cupboards for a French press, and then deliberating over mug choices as I waited for the water to boil.

Mostly, I avoided the conversation at the kitchen table. I had other things on my mind.

For starters, I'd broken a spell. A magical spell, cast by a magic-wielding witch.

Sure, I'd almost committed an assault on a person I was beginning to consider a friend in order to do it, but I'd done it. It was my first, almost-intentional magic.

Also, I'd seen the effects firsthand of what my magic—the magic I'd accidentally released into the wild in its raw and reusable form—could do. Miles had probably been exaggerating when he'd said he could have slept away his twenties if we hadn't woken him.

But what if he'd slept for a week? What if no one had noticed his absence? Or they'd noticed too late?

Humans needed food and water to survive, and I

assumed that magical humans had those same needs. How long before a person died from dehydration? And how horrifying would that be as a method of death? Would there be dreams of wandering the Sahara, parched and desperate for a drink? Or did magical sleep exempt one from dreams?

"You going to plunge the coffee?" Miles asked.

Instead of answering, I delivered it to the table along with three mugs. A sturdy, dark blue mug for Bastian. One with a snarky saying for Miles. And mine was bright and cheerful, because I needed a little lift, more than I'd be getting from the caffeine inside the cup.

I fetched cream from the fridge, splashed a generous dollop in my cup, because today was a day for splurges, and then passed it to Miles. "What have you come up with?"

"Hanna is almost definitely Rachael and Bartholomew's daughter," Miles said, as Bastian plunged the coffee and poured for everyone. "I was putting together a case for a mystery child, so I've got a birth date, a guardian from Rachael's will, as well as some information about the girl's education. All of the information I gathered is consistent with what we know about Hanna."

"Except her name," I murmured. Mostly because I was having difficulty reconciling the shy woman I'd met at Magic Beans with a coldly calculating killer.

"That's easy enough to change, and that's assuming she's done it legally. There are even more ways to do it illegally." Bastian returned my curious gaze with an innocent one. "Or so Miles says."

I turned to Miles. "How did she zap you?"

He blushed, the combination of dark stubble and pink cheeks making him look like an overgrown kid. "In my defense, the mystery child was only one of several avenues I was pursuing. Bartholomew was a thoroughly unpleasant person, who was disliked by a large number of people, which makes for loads of research."

"She knocked on his door." Bastian was watching Miles as he spoke. "And he let her in. Even though she was scheduled at Magic Beans. Even though she had no reason to be in his apartment."

And if she just showed up on his doorstep, that raised another question. "How did she know where you lived?"

"She shouldn't have," Bastian replied.

Now beet red, Miles said, "Fine. I might have had a little crush on Hanna, which may have slowed the functioning of my gray matter." He shot Bastian a defiant look. "You've had her coffee. Do you blame me?"

I blinked at that. Hanna was gorgeous if you looked beyond her mouse disguise, but Miles had fallen for her because of her coffee-making skills? That was new.

"She brought me a drink, a decaf vanilla latte." He bit his lip. "It was really good."

"And laced with a sleeping potion."

Miles crossed his arms. "I didn't know that at the time."

Poor Miles. That was incredibly gullible, but his sweetly innocent behavior might have saved him. "What if you'd questioned her? Asked her how she knew where you lived? Asked her why she'd come to your apartment?"

"Well, I wasn't completely checked out. She said she was stopping off on the way home and had brought me a thank-you for giving her a chance." He pinched the bridge of his nose. "Obviously, it didn't occur to me that she had a few hours left on her shift."

"Or that a normal employee wouldn't know where you lived." Because that really was stalker-level creepy for a normal, nonmurdering employee. For a murderer, though? It seemed like common sense to have an eye on all the investigative players.

"Rub it in some more. It wasn't bad enough waking up to find you waving around a knife."

I frowned at him. "It was a tiny knife, and I wasn't waving it. Also, you're welcome for waking you up."

"Ah, yeah, thanks for that."

I shot him a relieved smile. "I'm just thankful that there was no actual assault or blood involved. So what did you two come up with? Is there someone else Hanna might be after?"

Miles was looking steadier, so we needed to get a move on soon.

"Her motives appear revenge-based," Bastian said. "A father who didn't acknowledge her, a woman who could be seen as breaking up her parents' marriage."

"Or worse, precipitating her mother's death." Miles wrapped both hands around his mug. "I think Hanna's mom might have killed herself."

Oh, wow. That poor little girl.

"I really hope that's not the case." I paused, considering the ramifications if Miles's suspicions were true. "But if you're right, Miles, then who would she blame besides Cammi and Bitters?"

Who did a child blame for a parent's suicide?

When neither Miles nor Bastian had an answer, I ventured a guess. "She'd blame her mother, to some degree, don't you think? I know that's not helpful, but I do think—"

Bastian held up a hand, silencing me. "Miles, where is Rachael buried?"

"Oh, no. No, no, no. She wouldn't do that." Miles hopped to his feet and jogged to his office.

"Do what?" I asked. Because, really, whatever it

was, however appalling, of course she would do it. The woman had murdered two people. There probably wasn't much she wasn't capable of.

Miles returned with his laptop. "I've got everything on here. Just give me a second."

"If everything is on your laptop, then what's with all the piles of papers?" I asked, diverted momentarily from Hanna's potential evil purpose by the fascinating workings of Miles's mind.

"The physical representation of the data helps me to draw connections." He searched through the data on his laptop and after several seconds gave us the name of a cemetery. "What time is it?"

"It's not even six yet," Bastian said as he tapped on his phone. "We have a little over an hour. Sunset isn't until after seven."

"And we care about sunset why?" I asked. I had my suspicions, but my suspicions were crazy.

"There's a possibility Hanna wants to speak with her mother," Bastian said as he tapped away on his phone.

"Her dead mother," Miles said, as if that part hadn't been abundantly clear.

I looked between both men, at their concerned expressions. "That sounds like a bad idea."

"Very," Miles agreed as he continued to type on his computer. He stopped and waved over Bastian.

"Come here and log into this site for me. I can't get through the firewall."

"What in the world are you two doing?" I asked. Miles with his firewall and Bastian tapping away on his phone, they were definitely up to something.

"I'm looking for a decent ritual for calling forth the dead," Miles explained as Bastian logged him into some secret website. "It's forbidden, so it's not like I can just do an internet search."

Calling forth the dead? That sounded bad. Very bad. At least this community of magic people I'd newly joined were smart enough to recognize that something like "calling forth the dead" was a bad idea. Always a silver lining.

"And why do you need that? Shouldn't you be looking for a ritual on how to stop someone from calling forth the dead?"

"I'm scoping out the necessary supplies."

Supplies? To call forth a dead person? Probably best not to ask what those were, because if he started talking eye of newt and tongue of bat or some such nonsense, I'd... Well, I had not an inkling what I'd do. But that was just disgusting.

I turned to Bastian, who had finally put his phone down. "I was checking on Delilah and working on backup. Sabrina's in and she's picking up supplies Bethann recommended."

"Bethann?" Miles looked up from his internet search. "That's an odd choice."

Bastian shook his head. "Not everything is about coffee, Miles. Bethann has a knack for working with crystals and herbs. You should send her your list. She might have some ideas for countering Hanna's ritual."

It occurred to me that we were making an awful lot of assumptions. "What if Hanna isn't trying to reach out to her mom? What if she has another victim in mind?"

And we were dithering here, doing research on forbidden rituals, while Hanna might be hurting another person. Probably using *my* magic.

Miles handed a note to Bastian with a short list on it. "That's for Bethann." He scribbled down a few items on the pad in his hand and then lifted it. "This is how we'll know for sure. A few ingredients for the ritual that can't be sourced from a local garden, so will have to be purchased."

"Perfect." Bastian folded the note and put it in one of his many pockets. "We just need to check stock at the four possible suppliers. If any of them have had a recent rush on these items, then chances are good Hanna's target is her mom."

I peered over Miles's shoulder at the list. "Why wouldn't she purchase her supplies on the internet?

That seems like the smart move, since it would be harder to trace."

Miles shook his head. "Quality issues. Shipping can be tricky, so you'd want to source as much locally as possible. Product that stores can't source locally, they'll screen for efficacy before placing it on the shelves."

That might explain how a city of Boise's size could support four specialty magic supply stores.

We split up the retailers—whose numbers and websites were easily searchable on the internet, unlike Magic Beans—and called the stores.

We reconvened a few minutes later and discovered that of the five items on Miles's list, four had been purchased in large quantity at three different stores over the last three days.

"The store clerk I spoke with mentioned the same customer also bought a large quantity of frankincense, everything in stock. She was baffled as to why anyone would need such a large amount." I shook my head at Miles and Bastian's unasked question. "Before you ask, she couldn't describe the customer."

"My shop mentioned she also bought all of the dried lavender in stock in addition to their entire stock of dittany." Miles shook his head. "Bastian, any thoughts about the quantities she's buying?"

"To beef up the ritual? Amplify it?"

That sounded...not good. "You two need to explain what calling forth the dead means exactly."

"On the way," Bastian replied. Turning to Miles, he said, "You're good?"

"I think so." He stood without wobbling, proving his assertion true. He closed his eyes and touched his nose without hesitation, then stood on one foot without swaying like a drunk. "Yep. I'm good."

It was all a little too much like a sobriety test. Which meant he'd basically been drunk on that sleeping potion.

"He's not driving, right?" I asked Bastian in a low voice.

"I'm standing right here. And no, I shouldn't drive." He gathered his laptop case, slipped on his shoes, and said, "Ready. Let's go."

He wasn't fit to drive, but he was fine to confront a murderer. Hmm.

After locking his door, Miles slung an arm around my shoulders. As we followed Bastian back to his car, he said, "So calling forth the dead... Usually, it's about reaching beyond the veil and communicating with the recently dead. Sometimes it's about bringing that spirit back for a chat."

"Completely forbidden," Bastian said as he clicked his key fob and unlocked the Crosstrek. "For a variety of reasons, not the least of which is disturbing a sleeping spirit and opening up a channel for less friendly beings to cross over."

Less friendly beings? I stutter-stepped.

Miles squeezed my shoulder, steadying me.

Less friendly beings were bad enough, but what did it mean that Hanna was going big with her ingredients?

"You said that you think Hanna is trying to amplify this ritual. To what end?"

"Physical manifestation is my best guess," Bastian said.

This time I didn't need Miles to prop me up since we'd reached the car. I called shotgun and melted into the front seat.

A zombie? A corporeal ghost? Something worse? Although zombies and corporeal ghosts weren't exactly a day at the candy shop.

What were we walking into? How dangerous was the physical manifestation of a deceased person's spirit...or the less friendly beings that might hitch a ride with it?

Then again, did I really want to know the answer?

Probably yes, given the fact I was headed to meet whatever it was that Hanna was calling forth.

Maybe no, because I'd prefer to stay inside the confines of the car and not jump out in abject fear to run all the way home.

"Can I return my witch card?" I asked the world at large.

But the world wasn't there to answer, only Miles and Bastian.

They wisely refrained from comment.

14

Bastian, Miles, and I weren't headed to the cemetery, thank goodness.

Not yet, at least, so I had a little time to mentally prepare. I was going with that plan, and not the plan where I focused on how scary Hanna and whatever she was retrieving from beyond the veil might be. I liked my sanity, and I liked to at least pretend that I was brave.

First, we stopped at Magic Beans.

"It's on the way, and Sabrina is meeting us here," Bastian explained as he parked.

Bethann was behind the counter with a strawberry blond barista I hadn't met yet. His name tag read JONATHON.

He lifted a hand in greeting as he steamed milk. Jonathon didn't look like the world was about to end, so either he didn't know what was happening or I was potentially overreacting.

Bethann joined us as we marched toward the back of Magic Beans to the office. The four of us got a few odd looks from the patrons, but again, no one looked like the apocalypse was imminent, so maybe everything would be just fine.

Once we'd all filed into Bastian's office and the door was closed firmly behind us, Bethann let loose with more than a handful of harsh words.

"I'm going to kill her," Bethann said. "Chop her up into little pieces and use her as fertilizer in my garden."

I blinked at her in shock. Not that I knew her well—we'd only been introduced today—but her outburst seemed at odds with the easygoing, smiling woman from earlier.

"Bethann, watch it," Miles said. "You're upsetting Lina."

Hands on hips, she replied, "Yeah, well, that stupid witch Hanna is upsetting me, so what are you going to do about that?"

The exterior door of the office opened, and Sabrina stepped in with a cloth bag clutched in her hand. "I stopped by Bethann's to grab some supplies. What did I miss?"

Bethann snatched the bag, retrieved two small velvet pouches, then handed it back. "Looks good. It would be better if you arrive before she starts. Better yet if you get there before her ritual prep."

"That's unlikely at this point," Bastian replied. The moment we'd entered his office, he'd beelined to the bookshelves behind his desk. He spoke now from a squatted position in front of them.

"Well, maybe you should get a move on." Bethann's tart comment went unnoticed by Bastian, because he was studying the contents of the shelf intently.

Bethann rolled her eyes, then proceeded to hand out the contents of the velvet pouches—two stones, one from each small velvet bag—to Sabrina, Miles, and me. Sabrina and Miles pocketed them without question.

I looked at the two black stones in my hand and said, "Uh, what am I supposed to do with these?"

"Just put them in your pocket," Bethann replied. "They might help."

The stones felt cool in my hand. They didn't feel special or seem to have any sort of woowoo properties that I could identify. "Help with what?"

Bethann looked at me with a curious expression.

Sabrina patted my back. "She's a sleeper. No education, recently joined the community."

Information I was certain the entire magical community would know by now, given how small Bastian claimed the group to be. But it seemed the local representatives of the ICWP knew how to keep investigations and the accompanying details under their hat.

"Ah. They're shungite and jet. Stash them in a pocket. You'll know if you need them. As for *what* they'll help with..." She peered at me, then smiled. "You're going to a cemetery. I'll let you use your best judgment."

"So, a plan?" Miles directed this question at Bethann, not Bastian. "What are you thinking?"

Interesting that he asked her, since Bastian was usually the one calling the shots. Then again, Bastian was scanning his secret journals and paying us very little attention. He'd already popped the locks on at least four or five volumes and then replaced them after flipping through a few pages.

"Based on the list you gave me," Bethann replied, "I'm pretty sure she'll use a protection circle as the foundation for the ritual. That means, you have to either prevent her creating it or tear it apart."

"We know that much," Sabrina said with an annoyed huff. "No other words of wisdom, oh ye of great crystal and herb wisdom?"

"That's all I got. But hey, I brought the protection stones." She pointed to the bag full of items from her house. "And let you raid my personal supply stash. I'm still pretty awesome."

Miles poked his nose in the bag. "Thanks."

"Did anyone tell the newbie witch not to mess with the circle?" Seeing Miles and Sabrina's sheepish expressions, she turned to me and said, "Don't touch the protection circle. Not without any training."

I nodded. "Got it."

But this didn't reassure Bethann, because she replied, "Maybe you should skip this one?"

That sounded like a fabulous idea.

Looked like Bastian had finally decided on a book. He stood and stepped away from his mini library with one tucked under his arm. Not everything fit into those cargo pants pockets of his.

"Not an option." His tone implied that he wished it was. "Hanna is likely using Lina's magic, in part, to power the ritual."

Bethann's eyes grew round. "Oh." She blinked. "Right. Well, then I'll leave you to it. Be safe. And, not that it needs saying, but...try not to let anything cross the veil."

Anything? Not anyone? I thought we were trying to prevent Hanna from calling her mom forth.

But then I recalled the "less friendly beings" reference Bastian had made earlier. I felt like a kid who'd been told that monsters really did live under the bed, and, yes, they might grab your ankle, maybe even eat you.

But Bethann was already gone, back to the front

of the store to serve coffee, and everyone else was headed out the back door.

I bumped into Miles as he stopped suddenly. "It'll be a tight fit in the Crosstrek, assuming we're returning with a certain killer in custody."

"I've got the Suburban today," Sabrina said. "We'll take mine."

Which was how the four of us ended up in an older black Suburban that smelled faintly of dog, Bastian riding shotgun, Miles and I in the second row seating.

After we'd settled ourselves, I asked, "Why do you own a car large enough to transport a small army?" Maybe this was the unofficial prison transport for ICWP, because Bastian's little Crosstrek didn't seem suited for the purpose.

And with any luck, we would be transporting a particular prisoner this evening.

Was it hot in here? Jeans, a sweater and a light jacket had seemed about right earlier, but all of a sudden, I felt the need to divest a layer. Maybe two.

But I wasn't panicking, because panicking was for... Well, people who experienced fear, and fear seemed reasonable about now.

Sabrina snorted as she whipped through traffic. "You haven't heard yet? I'm the resident crazy dog lady."

As a woman who'd always wanted but never had

pets, I hadn't a clue what a crazy dog lady was, only that I wasn't one.

What I did know? I was a much, much safer driver than Sabrina. Also, I missed all the mirror-checking and the proper hand positioning that I'd become accustomed to over the last few days.

"Since you're too polite to ask," Miles said, "she's got three German shorthaired pointers and an occasional extra."

Huh? We were still talking dogs? We'd almost sideswiped a pickup.

And Bastian was in the front seat, completely Zenned out, not even noticing our multiple near misses.

What was he doing that had him so calm?

I leaned forward to find that he'd opened the journal he'd brought with him. It was resting in his lap as he read the handwritten pages.

The Suburban swerved erratically, but Bastian's eyes never left his book.

Sabrina was trying to kill us before Hanna could, Miles thought it was all a great joke, and I was about to have a heat stroke in October in Boise, Idaho.

I stripped off my sweater.

"Anyone want to clue me in as to how the quiet new girl turned out to be a serial killer?" Sabrina asked.

I fanned myself and practiced some deep breathing. Bastian ignored her question, so it was left to Miles to answer.

"She's not a serial killer. I'm not that much of an idiot."

"Not saying you are. Not saying you're not... Just that I'd have hired her in a heartbeat, too. She makes a mean latte and from the look of bliss on the boss's face every time he takes a sip of her coffee, she does a plain black pretty well, too."

We were pulling into the parking lot of the cemetery, and they were talking about lattes? And plain blacks?

"Coffee? Really? Now?" I might have yelled. And I was still hot, which was a problem because I couldn't exactly remove my long-sleeve tee; it was my last layer.

Bastian finally—finally!—looked up from his book. "We're looking for an old pickup truck, single cab, dark blue." Bastian pointed as Sabrina drove through the lot. "There."

Of course she'd arrived before us. I fanned my face.

We'd had to wake Miles, then get him sober enough to talk through what Hanna's next steps might be, then confirm that information, then gather supplies, pick up Sabrina...

Good grief. There better not be a pissed-off zombie mama in the cemetery.

I fanned harder.

"You okay over there?" Miles asked.

I didn't answer, just hopped out of the car now that we were stationary. I needed fresh air. "We're sure she can't complete the ritual before sunset?" I asked, once Sabrina, Miles, and Bastian had all exited the car.

"Set up, yes," Sabrina said. "The actual calling forth, not so much. Sunset is necessary for that part. Right, Bastian?"

He pulled his nose from his still-open journal and snapped it shut. "The veil can't be pierced in full light."

I blinked and the book was gone. As in, disappeared. "Did you just stash a full-sized journal in your cargo pants?"

Bastian frowned, like he didn't understand the question.

"Oh, yeah." Sabrina shot me a toothy smile. "Magic pockets. You didn't think he was wearing those as a fashion statement, did you? Although, you know, Bastian just might."

"Enough. The pants are off limits."

I coughed. Or laughed. Or gasped. All of those things. Also, I was still warm, and the air around me was sharp. I probably wasn't suited to bad-guy hunting.

Candy making, that was my jam. *That* was what I

should be doing. Making caramels and chocolates and hard candies.

Not chasing after some murderer intent on calling forth her dead mother from beyond the veil.

We were steadily approaching the cemetery gates, when I saw the sign announcing that visiting hours concluded at sunset. I pointed. "Um, we can't go in there. It's closed to the public after dark."

Three sets of eyes looked at me with varying degrees of pity and concern. My brain wasn't accustomed to functioning under this kind of pressure. Candy-making pressure, yes. Difficult-client pressure, sure. But spirits...or worse? Hard pass. No. Nope.

I didn't blame my brain. It liked living, so it was coming up with any excuse to not enter the cemetery.

"Maybe we should leave her in the car?" Miles mumbled.

"If we do, you know that'll guarantee that we need her," Sabrina replied. "With her wild magic juicing Hanna's ritual, chances are good she'll come in handy."

She shot a questioning glance at Bastian. Looked like he had the final say. "I'm ninety percent certain we'll need her."

Ninety percent was good. That meant there was a ten percent chance that I'd be nothing more than a decorative ornament this evening. For once in my life, I was good with being arm candy.

"I'm good. Minor brain glitch. All good. I'm in." The babbling should have been a clue I wasn't, in fact, "good" but they took me at my word and were already headed toward the entrance.

I could do this.

I fanned my face frantically and then hurried to catch up.

Does anyone know where the grave is?" I whispered to three backs.

Bastian led the group, Miles and Sabrina followed behind, and since the sidewalk was only wide enough for two, I brought up the rear all by my lonesome.

I was good with that. Being the last one to arrive when approaching a murdering witch intent on calling forth the dead seemed like the best of a bad situation.

One positive to our stroll through the cemetery was that my moving feet seemed to be easing my panic. I'd lost the need to fan myself, and I felt like my head was screwed on a little straighter.

"The fire's your first clue," Sabrina replied.

I should have expected a snarky response from

her, especially given the fact that when I bothered to lift my head and look around, there was actually a flame visible.

"Yeah, witching 101, fire, water, earth, air—all important in the big rituals. But fire's helpful, because it's highly visible in the dark. Especially, in a wide-open public area. Hint, hint." Then she pointed, in case I'd missed the telltale signs of a ritual circle.

A single flicker of light was joined by another and then another. Three flickering flames were now ahead and slightly to the right of us, flames that loudly pronounced Hanna's location in the diminishing light of the cemetery.

"Okay, fine," I whispered. "I see them."

"Hard to miss, right?" Sabrina said. "With a little training, you'll be able to spot obvious, well-lit clues in the dead of night without the aid of a more experienced witch."

"Cute," I muttered.

And while she was being flip, she did remind me that training was in my near future. Training with Great Aunt Sophia, unless I was wrong, and she wasn't my family's witchy mentor.

But there was a massive hurdle to be navigated before I had to consider the various awkward and unpleasant ramifications of training with my eccentric great aunt.

That hurdle was a two-time killer with a knack for making coffee.

And there I went with the sweating again. Nerves served a vital function—fear was a mechanism of self-preservation, and I liked living—but this was getting ridiculous.

Just as I was contemplating the necessity of my last layer—who needed modesty?—Bastian began mumbling words I didn't understand.

"What—" But Sabrina had already skipped ahead to stand next to Miles.

Bastian continued to mumble, in German if I had to guess, and I trailed along behind, wondering what the heck Bastian was up to and hoping I was capable of whatever this evening would require of me.

I didn't have long to ponder the uncertainties of our adventure, because tension began to build in the air. At first, I thought it was due to our increasing proximity to Hanna. We'd steadily gained ground on the four flame points that were now no longer so distant.

But then I realized the center of that power was nearer. Very near. Right in front of me.

Bastian.

The words he spoke remained unintelligible, gaining in neither volume nor speed, but they were the source of the energy I felt around us.

The air crackled. It snapped, as if electricity ran through it. But this was no electrical storm. This was the biggest, showiest magic I'd experienced since being outed as a witch.

I could feel the pulse of power in my fingers and my toes. My scalp prickled. The hair on the back of my neck stood at attention and my entire body shivered. Not in fear, because this was Bastian's magic.

I'd stopped in my tracks, awestruck by the intimate feel of Bastian's power washing over my entire body, which meant my merry band of magic friends had left me behind.

Hurrying to catch up, I returned to the group as we closed in on Hanna.

She stood ten feet away, not in the center of the circle she'd created, but just outside it. That seemed strange to me, but I didn't have time to ponder the implications, because Sabrina grabbed my hand. She'd already linked hands with Miles.

Bastian remained alone, untouched, slightly ahead of us.

We moved off the path, inching closer to Hanna, to her circle, to the grave inside it.

Sabrina, Miles, and I came to a stop at the edge of the protective circle Hanna had created around her mother's final place of rest. We were on one end, she on the other. And Bastian? Bastian had disappeared.

Neither Miles nor Sabrina seemed unduly concerned by his absence, so I wouldn't worry. He was fine. He must be, because the surging pulse of his power was still all around us.

The circle near my toes taunted me with the innocence of its constituent parts: salt, herbs, and dried flowers. I'd been told not to disturb it, and yet I sensed no danger. Nothing emanating from it.

I glanced to my left to find Sabrina eying the perimeter much as I was. Miles, however, had his eyes trained on Hanna.

As I looked at her, I expected some response to us, but she was busy chanting. Or calling? As in calling forth her dead mother?

She didn't seem worried about us, which definitely worried *me*.

Movement glimmered in the corner of my eye. When I turned, I expected to see Bastian, but there was no one. Nothing but an extinguished candle. Smoke rose in a lazy wisp from the wick.

Where there had been four flames spread equidistant around the circle, now only three remained. Was this the deconstruction of the circle that Bethann had mentioned in the office earlier this evening? I hoped so, because dusk was falling. And if it was, how was Bastian managing it? Where was he?

Another flame died, this time as I watched. It

was as if a localized wind, one pinpointed on the flame's location, puffed it out of existence.

As my gaze traveled to the two remaining sources of fire, I realized that there were representations of the three other elements on the circle as well: a potted plant with trailing vines for earth, an arrow with an old-fashioned stone or flint head for air, and a silver bowl filled with blue stones and clear liquid for water.

My study of the elemental objects distracted me from the third flame's demise, but the fourth went out with much more fanfare. As the light faded, Hanna's attention finally fell to Sabrina, Miles, and me.

Mostly me.

Only me.

We made eye contact, and it hit me. All of the earlobe gazing, the avoidance of direct eye contact, was because of *this*.

It started with an odd sensation of familiarity. Almost like déjà vu, except deeply unpleasant.

The familiarity wasn't one of place or situation. It was the familiarity of person.

It was like catching sight of myself in a mirror out of the corner of my eye. There was an instant unexpected recognition of a human who wasn't me and yet at the same time *was* me.

When I looked into her eyes, I saw a distorted

image of myself. And I also saw what she'd done. Every bit of it.

In her eyes, I saw that she'd used my magic to kill someone.

This woman was no mouse. Not even close.

She was a vengeful murderer.

"Lina," she acknowledged me, but none of the others.

Sabrina's fingers squeezed mine and then my other hand was grasped by Miles. While I'd been locked in a creepy stare down, Miles had flipped behind Sabrina and me to complete a circle.

A buzz of awareness traveled through me. Different from the pulse of Bastian's power that still surrounded us but with the same electric zing. Magic.

The three of us huddled on one side of the circle, Hanna on the other, and I waited. We were on the cusp of some event. But that was wrong, because Bastian had extinguished the flames. He'd disrupted the ritual before the sun had completely set.

Bastian appeared to the left of us. It was as if he'd stepped forward from behind a curtain. Then the thrum of his magic faded.

"You're too late." Hanna stood opposite us, exuding confidence.

"I don't see the departed Mrs. Bitters," Sabrina

said. "Do you guys?" No one answered, and she kept talking. "I think that means we're not too late."

Flippant as her words were, Sabrina's hand clung tightly to mine. Did she sense the same thing I did? That something was coming.

I scanned the circle but saw nothing untoward. Still, the feeling remained. A sense of waiting, an eerie anticipation.

Hanna stepped away from the circle. A foot, then two feet, then three.

Miles broke the heavy silence. "There's a reason we don't reach beyond the physical world with our magic. It's wrong to disturb the dead in their eternal sleep."

Hanna halted her retreat. "And if I want to disturb her? If she doesn't deserve to sleep peacefully?"

I couldn't believe that she'd replied. She was actually going to talk to us about her mother and her murderous motivations. Why?

Maybe feeling unheard or misunderstood had spurred her to kill, and she was keen for a captive audience.

Or maybe she was just passing time. Diverting us.

Miles took her question literally and replied, "Every spirit deserves to rest."

And that's when things got nasty.

Hanna jerked as if a tether attached to the core of her body had been yanked. And then she screamed.

If witches got their power from emotion, maybe now was the time to be scared of the power Hanna had, because she was livid.

I wasn't sure what had set Hanna off. Not at first.

The air groaned. It moaned in distress.

But then again, maybe it wasn't the air. Maybe it was the vacant-eyed woman leaning against the late Rachael Bitters's gravestone.

She was the cause of Hanna's rage.

Hanna shrieked, giving voice to the small abandoned child that still lived within her.

My gaze pinged between the enraged witch and the pale figure propped against what I realized must be her own headstone, because the woman could be no other than Rachael Bitters.

The protest on the tip of my tongue—but a spirit can't cross over if the circle's not complete!—died.

However it had happened, whatever we'd done wrong, Rachael Bitters's spirit had been called forth from across the veil.

16

Rachael Bitters's gaze caught mine, and I realized I'd incorrectly assumed her stare was vacant. Unfixed, yes. But vacant implied that no one was home, and I saw intelligence there.

She might be staring off into the distance, but this was a woman in pain. Unsettled, set adrift in a world where she no longer belonged, trapped in a body that anchored her to a place she shouldn't be.

In the chaos of Rachael's appearance and Hanna's emotional outburst, Miles, Sabrina, and I had maintained our linked-hands connection, but we'd moved further from the circle. We'd stumbled back several feet, surprise and self-preservation triggering an instinctual response to flee.

Hanna's flight instincts had kicked in, as well. Perhaps bringing her mother to this place to be tortured by her incompatibilities with the physical world had been her ultimate goal. Perhaps she'd intended to torment the woman further, but recognized—finally—that she was outnumbered.

Whatever the reason, she'd fled, leaving her mother trapped on this plane.

Hanna wouldn't get far. Bastian was after her and gaining. That running habit he'd mentioned looked to be paying off. I also had faith in his takedown skills. He'd snapped a pair of cuffs on me faster than the eye could track, and I was sure he'd do the same to Hanna.

Which left Rachael.

By this point, my fear of the embodiment of Rachael's spirit had diminished. We were easily within six feet of her, and she hadn't moved. She hadn't threatened us or even looked at us. She stared into space and expressed her agony in the only way it seemed she could, with pitiful sounds.

It made me sick that her own family had done this to her.

Sabrina tugged us closer to the circle.

"Wait." The word I'd intended to utter came from Miles. "We can't cross the circle. It's still intact."

Sabrina's grip on my hand didn't ease. "Bastian undermined the integrity when he extinguished the four points of fire. We can just walk through...with a little confidence."

"Please." He sounded exasperated. "Not every problem can be solved with bluster and balls."

While Bastian chased a self-absorbed killer and Sabrina and Miles bickered like siblings, Rachael Bitters suffered.

Whatever her choices in life, however she'd treated her daughter during her life, in death she deserved peace. A peace her daughter intended to snatch away.

She needed to be set free.

Miles and Sabrina's argument escalated but came nowhere near drowning out the pitiful sounds Rachael's spirit made.

"Stop!" I yanked my hands free in case words weren't enough to get their attention. "We can't walk through together, so how do we breach the circle?"

"We *can* walk through," Sabrina insisted.

"We can't," Miles snapped. "Not without someone getting hurt. We need to take it apart." He glared at Sabrina. "The flames weren't enough. We need to deconstruct the foundation."

The foundation of the circle? Seriously?

"We aren't talking about a building here. What does that mean?" Even though we were huddled close together, my tone was strident. I could barely think over Rachael's cries.

"The circle's drawn with a mixture unique to the

ritual and the witch. The drawn circle is the foundation."

"Okay, so we brush away the herbs and stuff." I knelt and reached my hand out. "Ow!"

I blew on the pink tips of my fingers. It felt like I'd touched a hot burner on the stove.

Sabrina grimaced at my newbie mistake, then she and Miles knelt near the curved line on the grass. As they examined it, Bastian returned, towing a cuffed and eerily passive Hanna.

She came to a stop when Bastian did, standing completely still. She didn't struggle—couldn't, if my suspicions were correct—but her eyes flashed defiance.

Bastian muttered a few words, and I swear if Hanna could move that she would have killed him in that moment. Then he walked away, leaving her without a moment's hesitation.

He followed the edge of the circle to the side opposite where Miles, Sabrina, and I had gathered. The side closest to Rachael.

Then he began murmuring in the foreign tongue he used to work magic. His voice was low and soothing, his words flowing so smoothly it was almost as if he sang.

And Rachael listened. She quieted, her moans softening and then dying. Only the sound of Bast-

ian's words could be heard in the quiet of the cemetery now.

I let out a breath that I felt like I'd been holding
since I walked into the cemetery.

Freedom from Rachael's distressed cries brought
not only relief but also a flash of clarity. "If Hanna
used my magic to create this circle, shouldn't I be
able to take it apart?"

"Maybe. Hard to say. Probably worth a try,"
Miles said, but his attention was split between me
and Hanna, whom he eyed warily. After a shared
glance with Sabrina, he stood and stepped away
from the circle to stand guard near Hanna. "Be
careful."

I wasn't sure if that comment was directed at
Sabrina or me.

"What do I do?" I asked, watching the woman
who looked like a pale copy of the Rachael Bitters I'd
seen in photos.

At least now she seemed comfortable. Her
pained expression had eased along with her cries. So
long as Bastian didn't stop his soothing patter, hope-
fully she'd stay calm. My glance flicked to Bastian,
whose entire focus was on Rachael.

"Come closer and have a look." Sabrina scowled.
"But don't touch."

I knelt next to her, keeping my hands well away.
Magic was strange. My feet were easily as close—

closer, in fact, than my hand had been to the circle. But my toes weren't being singed.

"What do you see?"

I eyed the curving line of strewn ingredients in the grass. "A bunch of dried plants I don't recognize. Some purple flowers I'd guess are lavender. Rock salt." I leaned closer, then pulled out my phone and clicked on the flashlight app. "Huh. Sugar. There's definitely sugar mixed in."

Sugar looks a bit different from table salt, and also I didn't see why table salt would be included in addition to rock salt.

Sabrina made a sound of disgust. "Of course there is."

I understood her comment to be sarcastic, implying sugar was an uncommon ingredient. Hanna must have customized the circle around my magic. "Some of my cupcake topper is in there, isn't it?"

"Yeah. You can't feel it?"

I shook my head. I'd just hope that wasn't a problem. "So what do I do now?"

Bastian broke his chant to reply, "You sweep."

"What?" I didn't understand that at all.

"Oh, I get it," Sabrina nodded. "Like the trick with the knife. Got it, Bastian."

Which was a good thing, because the moment Bastian's magical lullaby had ceased, Rachael's agitation increased. He couldn't explain without sacrificing Rachael's temporary calm.

"Pay attention," Sabrina said. "You're sweeping away bad energy."

"I don't have a broom." The words sounded as idiotic out loud as they had in my head.

She muttered something disparaging about baby witches under her breath. "It's a metaphor, Lina."

"I didn't actually need the knife to cut the spell. I just had to think really hard about cutting and imagine it." I could do that...except with a broom...without having the broom. "Are you sure this will work?"

"Sure."

That wasn't promising, especially given the fact I'd burned my fingers already.

"You're sweeping bad juju away, and it happens to be right there." She pointed at the circle of salt, sugar, lavender, and herbs.

Which were all ingredients. Most of which I'd worked with before. Regularly even, given that salt and sugar were a part of almost every candy I made. I used lavender regularly, as well. My lavender-lemon drops were very popular.

This circle was just a recipe. One that had gone wrong and needed a little cleanup.

"Uh, stop if it burns."

"Got it." I didn't have it. Why had she mentioned burning?

I thought about sweeping, but then my brain wanted to know if I was using my fingers to actually sweep the materials away or if this effort was one hundred percent metaphorical and I was waving my hands around.

Since I'd actually planned to cut Miles and then hadn't needed to, I decided it was best to call this a truly physical act—just far enough away that I didn't get singed.

Sweep the debris aside...from a foot away, since I didn't want to watch my fingers burn like candles.

And now I couldn't even make my hand move, because I was thinking of my digits aflame.

A quick brush of bad ingredients. That was all this was. A quick brush of bad ingredients. A quick brush...bad ingredients.

My hand waved ineffectually in the air. Nothing. Nada.

I closed my eyes and tried again, thinking, "A quick brush of bad ingredients into the trash."

"Um, Lina?"

I opened my eyes to see Sabrina blinking at me.

"I don't suppose you know where exactly you sent Hanna's hex mix?"

"Hex mix?" I asked.

"The materials used to draw the— You know what? Never mind."

Glancing down at the circle, I discovered a large swath of the sweeping line was simply missing. The ingredients hadn't been brushed aside; they were gone.

"Now what?" I looked up. There was no longer any barrier between Rachael's spirit and the rest of the world, and yet she remained propped against her headstone.

Sabrina took my hand and pulled me through the gap I'd made.

I followed her closer to the passive Racheal, Bastian's voice still a backdrop to our efforts. But then she grabbed Rachael's hand. Her dead hand.

Worse, she looked at me as if I should take the woman's other hand. "The longer she's here, the harder she is to send back."

I didn't take the hint to hurry up. Instead, I dithered. Because dead person, dead person's hand, touching a dead person's hand... I shivered from the tips of my toes to the ends of my fingertips.

"Is that safe?" I whispered. As if Rachael might not hear me if I spoke quietly.

It wasn't clear if the woman understood anything happening around her, with the exception of Bastian's quiet, persistent patter.

"Sure." Her response was flippant, which gave

me pause. She scowled. "Probably. Maybe." She sighed, then said, "Honestly? I don't know. But she was called with your magic, so your participation is an important component to sending her back."

I looked to Bastian for reassurance, but he offered me none. His look was grim, and he couldn't exactly reply since his words were the only thing keeping Rachael calm.

I tried to catch Rachael's eye, but she was entranced by Bastian and his words. The calm expression she wore would evaporate the moment Bastian released her from the spell he'd woven. He'd captivated her, but it was only temporary.

Before I could change my mind, I clasped her hand.

And I was suddenly so very, very cold.

Rachael's fingers clutched at mine like claws digging into my flesh, and the ice that was hers became mine.

First my fingers, then my palm...my arm.

On some level, I realized this might be a bad outcome.

Someone joined our small circle—Miles, it was Miles—and for a moment, I felt a tiny prick of warmth. But then it was gone, swallowed by the cold.

Cold that had moved to my shoulder, my neck, my lungs. It ached to take a breath, and each exhalation pushed icy air through my body.

I tried to blink but even my eyeballs hurt as the frigid bite settled there, as well.

There was chatter. Words I couldn't follow, because I was just so very cold.

The quality of the air around me changed. Or perhaps it wasn't the air. Perhaps it was the cemetery and the people around me who'd changed.

They seemed insubstantial. As if they were made of mist and vapor. As if they had no substance.

I had a pleasant realization: the cold was gone. In its place...nothing. No feeling.

Not of hands clasping my own.

Not of ribs aching with each breath.

Not the burning pinpricks that accompanied overchilled limbs.

Numbness.

Perhaps this was what death was like? Sensation fading away, an impenetrable haze covering everything, the world turning into a ghostly imitation of itself.

I didn't want to die.

17

In my last moments, worries about Sticky Tricky Treats filled my head. I had no will and had done no estate planning. Who would run my beloved store? Would all my work be for nothing? Would Sticky Tricky Treats simply fade away?

When my final thoughts, moments before death, are of my business and not my loved ones, that might be a sign.

Definitely a sign.

A sign that I needed to get a life.

A sign that my life wasn't as fulfilled as I'd once believed.

It might also be a sign that I hadn't been on the cusp of death at all, because, truly, weightier matters should prevail...I hoped.

On the heels of that revelation, I felt the warm sensation of Bastian's hand encircling my own.

It was such a nice, pleasant, cozy—"Ow!"

All of a sudden, feeling returned to my body. And...*ow*. I hurt everywhere. I felt like I'd been hit by a bus. Or a linebacker.

"Hey, she said something!" Sabrina's worried voice came to me from out of the darkness.

Someone smacked my cheek, which prompted another expression of pain, this one more colorful than the last.

"Why isn't she opening her eyes?" Miles asked. "Do you think she has brain damage?"

Since I hadn't a clue my eyes were closed, I now made the effort to lift my heavy lids—yes, they ached, too—and a few salient facts were revealed.

I was lying on my back on the hard ground. Landing there might explain some of the aches I was currently experiencing.

Miles, Sabrina, and Bastian were all looming over me, which indicated they, unlike me, hadn't suffered a fall.

Finally, Rachael was conspicuously absent from my view.

"I'm not brain damaged." I propped myself up on my elbows. "Not any more than before."

Bastian cleared his throat. "Glad to hear it." His voice sounded funny.

"Rachael?" I asked.

"Sent back, beyond the veil." Sabrina looked...worried?

I pushed myself up to a sitting position. "And Hanna?"

Miles pointed.

A few feet away, Hanna stood utterly still. Whatever enchantment Bastian had slapped on her, it was a good one.

Miles and Sabrina gave me a last look then marched off to collect our murderer.

"Any chance you want to give me a hand up?" I stretched out a hand to Bastian.

He ignored it and sat on the ground next to me. "Maybe give yourself a minute."

"I feel fine. Really."

"Since you just came as close to crossing over to the other side as any living person in my experience, trust me when I say you should give yourself a minute."

Crossing over? "Wait, a living person can cross over?"

"No."

His abrupt, almost harsh, response had an unusual effect. I chuckled.

I couldn't help remembering my thoughts as I'd quite possibly edged toward death. I'd been worried about Sticky Tricky Treats—which was ludicrous.

Laughably so.

"Glad you find this amusing. It wasn't entertaining to watch. I didn't—" He scrubbed a hand across his face. "This should never have happened. Rachael shouldn't have been called after we extinguished the flames."

"Speaking of, I don't understand how you managed to put out those four candles."

"An incantation. One that stirred confusion and created a cover to conceal my actions."

"Oh. So you were there the whole time." I'm not sure why that made me feel better, knowing that when he'd disappeared, he hadn't really been gone.

"The whole time." There was a smile in his voice now that we weren't talking about my near-death experience.

"Back to the earlier question, how was Hanna able to call Rachael from the other side? Because I know you got those flames extinguished before sunset."

"Miles and Sabrina think maybe the call had already been made and the fall of sunset was the last component, so when we interrupted the ritual, even though it was before sunset, it was too late." He cleared his throat. "I just wanted to say... I wouldn't have brought you if I'd known it was going to be so dangerous."

I glanced at him, surprised. "I thought you

needed me here. Because Hanna was using my magic."

"Turned out, we did. We likely wouldn't have been able to make the link with Rachael that we needed to make in order to send her back."

It didn't escape my attention that he'd failed to address the inconsistency: needing me present and regretting including me.

Best not to mention it, since he wasn't keen to discuss it and this was the chattiest he'd ever been with me. So I asked a question that weighed on me. "Did she make it back? Is Rachael at peace again?"

"As much as she ever was." When I stared hard at him—because that was no answer at all—he added, "We don't know much about what lies beyond the veil. But she's been released from this place."

The fight-or-flight nerves that had me stripping off layers earlier were all gone, and the cold was creeping past my long-sleeved tee and into my skin. At least it was just the weather and not the other-worldly cold of the spirit world.

I shivered. "She didn't belong here, and I think it caused her pain—real, physical pain—to be here."

"It did." He removed his jacket and wrapped it around me. I was enveloped by the scent of Christmas and cuddles.

He spoke with such assurance about Rachael's pain, and it had been his words that had soothed her. It didn't take a great leap for me to draw a conclusion.

"That's what your lullaby did, wasn't it? You took her pain away with your words."

He blinked and then smiled. "My lullaby?"

"Well, it was in some foreign tongue, so I can't attest to the content, but it had a rolling, calming rhythm that reminded me of a lullaby. Or maybe a soothing chant."

"It was an incantation to help ease her suffering."

A light went off in my head. "That's what's in the journals! Incantations." And probably why there was decent security on his office.

"Yes."

I nudged him with my shoulder. "Wizards versus witches, the head versus the heart. Really, the difference is that you're a big research nerd and like to do magic homework."

He chuckled. "Sure."

Not that witches didn't have their own brand of homework. Potions and hex mixes that were prepared in advance. Research for rituals, as tonight's adventure had proven. Were witches and wizards really all that different?

"Are you feeling up to the walk back to the parking lot?"

I nodded. I'd been fine five minutes ago, but I

was glad for the brief interlude before facing the rest of the gang.

As he stood, I removed his jacket. I returned it, then extended my hand.

With great efficiency and not a bit of lingering, he helped me to my feet. He eyed me critically. "You're sure you're fine?"

"Yeah," Sabrina said as she approached, a gagged Hanna grasped firmly in one hand. "It's not every day that you come within a few feet of death."

"Feet?" Miles said. "Try inches. Just be glad Bastian isn't so uptight about wizard rules that he wouldn't join our circle."

Bastian had broken a wizard rule to help me?

I knew that his joining the circle had tipped the balance. It just made sense. I was losing touch, fading away. Then I'd felt Bastian's touch, and I was back again.

But I hadn't known that he was breaking the rules to do it.

Miles must have realized he'd made an error in admitting as much, because he shot Bastian a sheepish look and said, "Sorry, boss."

Sabrina jabbed Miles in the ribs hard. "We agreed not to mention the unmentionable thing that could get Bastian in trouble with his gran."

Bastian had a *gran*? He seemed the type to have a *grandmother*. Grans were sweet little old ladies who knitted more scarves than you could wear in two lifetimes and made your favorite cookies every time you visited.

Grandmothers, on the other hand, had perfect posture and told you that you'd used the wrong fork. Yep, Bastian seemed like the sort to have a grandmother.

But it also appeared that his "gran" wasn't a topic he cared to discuss. So I turned my attention to Hanna.

"Why is she gagged?" I posed this question as five of us followed the path back to the parking lot. Later, if I remembered, I'd ask how we'd avoided detection by the nonmagical security that the cemetery surely had in place.

"She kept on and on about the wrongs done her in her childhood and how the world was against her." Miles shrugged. "She was pushing Sabrina's buttons, so I thought it best to keep her quiet."

"Good thing, too," Sabrina said with a vicious look pointed at the woman she was none-too-gently dragging behind her. "If I had to hear any more about how it was so terrible to be raised by an older cousin, a woman who took her in and clearly adored her, or how her life was ruined by her father and his second wife, people she'd never even met, by the way, then I could not be held responsible for my actions."

Wow, someone had some strong feelings.

"Don't ask," Miles mumbled quietly.

But not quietly enough, because Sabrina replied, "Really, Miles? Because you think it's just fine to blame other people for your vicious, revenge-seeking, murderous actions?"

"Uh, no. I don't have any vicious, revenge-seeking murderous actions."

"Exactly!"

Sabrina's rant might not make complete sense, but the gist of it—that one is ultimately responsible for one's own actions—was fairly clear.

It made me wonder about her own background. Who was she trying so hard not to blame? Or what had she moved past?

I filed those questions away for a later day. A day when I hadn't met a ghost. A day when I hadn't come, per Miles, within inches of death.

"You know what?" I said as I climbed the front passenger seat of the Suburban. "I think I'm taking tomorrow off. Shutting the shop, calling it a family emergency or something, but definitely taking the day completely off."

Sabrina, who along with Miles had maneuvered Hanna into the second-row seating, said, "No need to shut the shop down. I'll babysit." She grinned over her shoulder. "Working at Sticky Tricky Treats doesn't completely suck. Besides, I could use another day to finish up my overhaul of your online ordering system."

I ignored the twinge of unease her words inspired and accepted her gesture for exactly what it was: a kindness.

A cranky kindness filled with backhanded compliments, but still a kindness. "Thank you, Sabrina."

18

Monday morning, two days later, I was having some very mixed feelings about letting Sabrina get her hands on my online ordering system.

She'd revamped it, all right. She'd even left me with a reference binder. After flipping through it, it seemed that it was simpler, more streamlined, than the system I had in place before.

But then I'd retrieved the orders for the day.

I had so many orders that my stock would be completely wiped out if I didn't get cracking cooking up candy every night well into the wee hours for the rest of the week.

Which was amazing, but also...wow.

I wanted to thank her and then strangle her.

And both of those feelings warred with each other right up until noon, when she appeared in the store.

"Heya," she said as she breezed in, walked behind the counter, and put an apron on.

"Um, hi?" To the best of my knowledge, Sabrina's tenure at Sticky Tricky Treats was over. She'd babysat the shop one more day on Saturday, and that should have been the end of her help.

"Look at you. You figured out how to print the orders." She made it sound like I had the tech skills of my Great-Aunt Sophia—in other words, none at all.

"What exactly did you do to my ordering system? You didn't—" I looked around the shop, checking to ensure no patrons were near. "You didn't use magic to boost my visibility, did you?"

She laughed. It was a bright, sparkling sound. The first genuine, snark-free laugh I'd heard from her. "No, I did not. There's no magic required when you have skills."

"And you have skills."

"Of course I do." She scowled, all traces of humor gone. "I told you I did."

I nodded. She had, I just... Well, I found it hard to trust, especially when it came to the shop, because the shop was my baby.

"So, yeah, I figured you'd want some help filling

online orders." If I wasn't mistaken, Sabrina was looking the smallest bit uncertain. "You know, now that your sales will be tripling and you're losing Lucy and everything."

"Wait—what?" Tripled sales? Losing Lucy?

"Yeah, she's put off telling you, because you're kind of hard to talk to about some things."

"Things like her quitting?" Because...yes! Yes, that would be hard to discuss. I couldn't lose Lucy.

Sabrina pointed a finger. "This is your fault. She adores you and working at the shop, and she didn't want to let you down, but—" She put her hands on her hips. "You do realize that students graduate, right?"

"But Lucy doesn't graduate until May!" I was pretty sure that was right.

Not that I'd asked, because asking meant facing the reality of losing my dependable, friendly, affordable help. I *liked* Lucy. Working with her was fun.

And there was that uncertainty again. "She graduates in December, Lina. And she really didn't have time to work here this fall, but she didn't want to let you down. So, uh, I told her that she could quit because I'd be working here."

I covered my face with my hands. I was the worst boss ever. When I looked up, I saw Sabrina looking at me. Waiting.

"You're going to work here?"

She bit her lip. Oh, yeah. That was uncertainty, clear as day. "If you hire me, I will."

I nodded. It would solve all my problems and give my overworked part-time employee the time she clearly needed to finish her degree. "I'll call her today and tell her not to come in for her next shift." I glanced at the pages of orders I'd printed out. "Assuming you're ready to start right away?"

"Yep. I like the hours here better than Magic Beans, and Miles has always been desperate to take over as head barista. I'll still work for Bastian a few evenings a week and as a fill-in."

A lightness filled me. I'd known in the back of my head that Lucy was a temporary solution to a long-term problem. Ideally, I'd have hired someone who was more committed to the business. And it didn't get much more committed than overhauling my entire online ordering system.

"All right then. Let's get to work. Your little revamp has put a massive dent in my stock, so we're going to be busy for the next few days."

I lifted a hand for a high five. I expected an eye roll in return, which I got, but she didn't leave me hanging.

Four hours later, with the shelves looking much thinner, the online orders from the weekend were filled. Sabrina hustled out the door, saying she still had a shift at Magic Beans this evening.

I expected a short burst of foot traffic, but nothing I couldn't easily handle alone, so I waved her cheerily on her way. She'd been great with the customers, and even though her attitude otherwise wasn't all rainbows and lollipops, she was fun to work with.

A few more hours, and I could close the shop... and then make more candy.

And also call Bryson.

The boost I'd felt from filling STT's large queue of online orders faded a little bit. I really should have called him on Saturday, but I'd been taking a vacay from life. A much deserved one, if I did say so myself.

I stopped fiddling with the display near the door when the jingle of bells alerted me to the first customer of the early evening rush.

I cut short my standard greeting as I saw who'd stepped through the door. "Bastian. Hello." A wide smile bloomed. I guess I was happy to see him.

"Hi." He looked a little nervous.

"You're not here to arrest me, are you?" I was kidding, but then again—he did look jumpy.

"No. Of course not. No, I was just... I thought you might like to know that everything with Hanna has been finalized."

My eyebrows flew up in surprise. "Finalized? How?"

"She's been processed and transferred to ICWP's Seattle branch. They're better equipped to house serious criminals pending trial than we are."

"That's a relief, just having her out of town."

He nodded. He examined me, looking for... something. "You're doing all right?"

"Yes. Fine, thanks." Which was when I remembered that I'd stolen one of his employees. One of his best employees. "Oh! Sabrina... Did she tell you she's going to work here?"

"Yes. That's no problem." He waved a hand dismissively, as if losing a barista with the much-sought-after feel was no big deal. "I'm glad she'll be helping out here. The hours are better for her, and she'll still be doing a little work at Magic Beans."

"I'm excited to have her. She's surprisingly good with customers, and she's already increased my online orders and streamlined the process on my end. My inventory automatically updates, and there's—" I shook my head. "The details aren't important. Let's just say she's made an amazing difference in a very short time."

He grinned. "Don't get used to it. She's incredibly productive when she has insomnia, but most of the time she's a little less like a superhero."

It occurred to me, as we chatted, that I'd miss seeing him. Without the excuse of an investigation, I wouldn't have a reason. And he'd already made it clear what he thought of wizards and witches mingling socially.

It made me sad, because Bastian was very much a man I'd like to get to know better.

"If I ask you a question, can you promise not to feed me the International Criminal Witch Police party line?"

"Okay." He squirmed. "Though I may not be able to answer at all."

"Uh-huh. So, would you really have charged me as an accessory to murder if I hadn't helped you?"

"Probably not."

"Bastian," I gently chided.

"All right. Truth? No, I wouldn't have. That would have been a gross miscarriage of justice. But I wasn't misrepresenting the possibility of that outcome. Technically, you could be charged as an accessory for providing the magical means of the murder."

"Uh-huh. So why did you do it?"

His cheeks pinked. "Why did I do what?"

"Twist my arm to help with the case."

He remained stubbornly silent.

"I know it was Miles and Sabrina's idea to include me, but you went along with it. Why?"

He shrugged. "I told you before, I needed proof of cooperation, something that demonstrated you'd aided the investigation."

"For who? You never mention your boss or your

chain of command." I crossed my arms. "Did you want to keep an eye on me?"

He'd admitted during the investigation that he'd placed magical protections of my shop, car, and home. He could have done that and walked away in good conscience.

"Tell me."

"Yes, I wanted to keep an eye on you, to make sure the killer didn't decide to tie up any loose ends. And what I said about having evidence of your cooperation is also true. I'm in charge locally, but I do report to a superior and am accountable for all of my decisions. But I also thought..." He cleared his throat. "I thought if you helped find the killer, it might help you, ah..." Color rose in his cheeks.

A light bulb went off. "You thought I'd feel less guilty about facilitating a murder."

He blinked. "Maybe. Not that I think you're responsible. You didn't even know magic existed."

"You sweet, sweet man." On impulse, I leaned forward and kissed him on the cheek.

But then, up close and personal with all the Christmas and cuddles scent, I couldn't help but go in for the hug.

He didn't linger after that hug. In fact, he practically ran out of the shop.

But I did get one promise out of him before he

left: if any other nefarious deeds were committed using the unaccounted-for cursed candy, he'd let me know.

19

I'm a witch." I leaned against my kitchen counter with my phone pressed to my ear as I waited for Bryson to reply.

Bastian had explained that family weren't supposed to discuss magic unless all the participating parties were inside the witchy circle of trust.

How did I know who was in that secret circle?

I was gambling that Bryson's frantic reaction to my vague inquiry about witches meant that he was.

I'd waited until Monday evening to call him, because I'd needed a few days off from life after my recent adventure in the witch world.

He sighed. "Yeah. I kinda figured when you started asking questions. Real subtle, by the way." He mimicked my voice. "What do you think about witches, Bryson?" His voice returned to its normal pitch. "And then you left me hanging. Vicious, cuz."

"What was I supposed to say? Apparently, most witches are spotted in their teens, maybe early twenties at the latest. Because I'm a late bloomer, I've been running around with magic for who knows how long, breaking who knows how many rules."

He chuckled. "Kills you, doesn't it? You're such a little rule follower. But none of that explains why you dropped a text bomb and then went radio silent."

I wasn't such a rule follower—except in comparison to him.

"I didn't mean to leave you hanging. There were extenuating circumstances." As I puttered around my kitchen, starting a batch of caramels I'd planned to make as a thank-you for Bastian, I gave him an abbreviated recounting of the last few days, starting with the accidental unleashing of my cursed candies into the world and ending with the capture of Hanna and Rachael's return to the spirit world.

"You really know how to make a splash. I'm glad you're safe—and not in jail." He paused, then in a quiet voice, said, "Tell me about this wizard Bastian."

Rather than bristle—it was not a coincidence that of all the new friends I'd mentioned, he'd landed on Bastian, the only wizard and the only person I was attracted to—I shared all of the thoughts that had been bouncing around unhappily in my head since I'd seen him last.

I was attracted to him, but he seemed to consider me completely off-limits. He could be gruff, but mostly was kind, considerate, and generous. Occasionally a little uptight, but overall a warm, caring guy.

When I was done, he said, "You're completely into this guy."

"I'm not...but I could be." I checked the temperature on my candy thermometer. Wouldn't do for it to get too hot.

He sighed again. "Here's the thing. Witches and wizards—"

"Bastian explained that we don't mingle."

"Eh. That may be true in Europe, or maybe it was when Bastian was a kid. Didn't you say he's old like you?"

"Cute. Just keep that up, and you'll be getting no candy from me for your birthday." Since Bryson loved all things sweet and was usually on a strict diet, his birthday was one of his allowed cheat days, and I knew he'd be waiting for my package of treats.

"Hey, now. Let's not be hasty. They say fifty is the new forty."

"I'm in my thirties, you jerk. And Bastian is barely in his forties. We're not *that* old."

Much more seriously, he replied, "No, but you're

old enough to know that prejudice exists everywhere. And you're also old enough to know you should make your own judgments about people, not relying on outdated social mores to rule your life. If you like this guy, then get to know him. Wizards can be quirky, but they can be cool."

"Aw. Are you being supportive of my dating life?" Because usually, Bryson liked to think of me as the Virgin Mary: untouched and untouchable, forever pure. That's how it seemed to me, since he'd been hypercritical of every man I'd ever dated.

"You deserve a good guy. And I think this Bastian guy might be okay."

I laughed as I turned off the burner on my stove. "You know that from the little I've said about him."

"Yeah, I do. But don't worry, I'll be asking around about him. If there's any dirt, I'm sure I'll dig it up. And I'll try to make it out to Boise on my next break."

Since Bryson's schedule was crazy, I figured I had until the end of hockey season before he showed up on my doorstep. By then, Bastian and I probably wouldn't even be talking. He was busy catching criminals and running a coffee shop; I was busy keeping Sticky Tricky Treats in the black.

"Um, Cuz? Don't you think it's time we talked about the elephant in the room?"

We'd covered my irregular introduction to

magic, the resolution of my first major magical blunder, and the new friends I'd made in the magical community—what was left? "Uh..."

"Great-Aunt Sophia."

"Oh, no." I lifted a hand to cover my eyes. "She's our family mentor. She's the one who's supposed to do my training."

"She is," Bryson agreed, much too cheerfully. "I suffered through her crazy, and now it's your turn."

"There is no possible way that I can leave town. It's October. That's my biggest month, Bryson. I run a Halloween-themed candy store, for goodness' sake."

"Which is hilarious, and you're finally in on the joke: witch with a Halloween candy shop." He snort-laughed.

"Ha ha. Seriously, I can't leave. And even once October is over, November, December, and early January are huge months for me. People eat and gift a lot of chocolate over the holidays."

"Right. I get that. I do actually pay attention when you wax poetic over STT. Even when you go on and on about accounts payable and marketing and online sales."

"You do not."

"I do. Anyway," he said, a note of satisfaction entering his voice, "you're just going to have to invite our darling great-aunt for a visit."

"Nooooo."

But all of my whining didn't change the reality of my situation. Crazy Great-Aunt Sophia would have to be invited. And knowing her, she'd come.

I thought becoming a witch made my life complicated. Well, my life path had just taken a hard left into the land of rabid eccentricity.

For more of Lina's witchy adventures, pre-order *Twisted Treats*!

Keep reading for an excerpt from Cate's humorous paranormal cozy mystery, *Adventures of a Vegan Vamp*.

EXCERPT: ADVENTURES OF A VEGAN VAMP

I died a little.

I wish I could say it was a blur, but it's a blank. A mystery.

I was an anxiety-ridden, overachieving, successful (and perhaps not entirely likable) professional—and human. I definitely started this story very human.

But now I'm none of those things.

This story is about the murder of that woman and catching the man who killed her. It's also about how I became a vampire and also a little about how becoming a vampire was the best thing that could have happened to me.

***

Why did my mouth feel like it had been stuffed

with cotton balls? I tried to swallow and almost threw up in my mouth.

Not good. Very not good. I held my breath and fought the urge to swallow again.

I needed to be absolutely still. Moving made me want to ralph, and I would never make it to the bathroom.

Even the thought of moving made my head pound with a vicious rhythm.

My eyelid cracked of its own volition and the pain at the base of my skull and behind my eyes ratcheted up. I carefully shut my eyes and lay very, very still.

Finally, after counting backward from a hundred, I started to feel myself drift away.

***

My eyelids popped open. I did a quick check for eyelid gunk, but my eyes were surprisingly clear of superglue funk. A buzzing energy filled me, not unlike a massive caffeine high. Not traditionally a morning person, that was more than a little surprising.

All of that energy was accompanied by a massive thirst that reminded me of the pitcher I'd filled earlier. I turned to my bedside table, planning to drain the pitcher—but it was already empty. Odd. I didn't remember waking up, and certainly didn't remember drinking an entire pitcher of water.

I made my way to the kitchen in search of liquids. I even considered braving some milk. But sanity returned when I remembered my earlier puke-fest. Water for now. After drinking three tall glasses, I filled a fourth glass and sat down at my computer. I needed to go to the doctor, preferably right now, while I still had the energy to get dressed and leave the house. Who knew how long that would last? And I needed a new doctor. My guy wasn't going to cut it. He didn't have weekend hours —and he just wasn't going to work.

Three rejections later, I'd exhausted the only options that fit my needs. Finding anyone with weekend hours, who was accepting new patients, and took my insurance, was apparently an impossible task. I tried to take a drink, but found I'd drained yet another glass of water. I stared at the empty glass. That was not normal.

I tried not to get frustrated, but I was on the clock. Who knew when my little energy boost would fade away, and I'd end up passed out in bed again for several hours?

With renewed determination, I scratched insurance off my list of requirements and kept searching. Five minutes later, I'd found a doctor who shared a clinic with several alternative medicine practitioners. Not sure how I felt about that, but she had weekend hours and the website declared, "New patients welcome." I wasn't holding my breath, because two other traditional doctors had said the same—but that didn't include new patients to be seen this weekend.

Also, I wasn't entirely sure what alternative medicine meant in the context of this practice. The two doctors on staff were both MDs, but it looked like the practice offered some other therapies. Maybe that meant they'd be open-minded about my weird symptoms? Or at least not assume I was starving myself intentionally. The thought was enough for me to dial the number.

"Doctor's office. How may I help you?" The chirpy voice on the line sounded helpful enough.

"I'm in urgent need of an appointment this week-end. Do you have any available?"

"Are you already a patient with us?"

I wanted to groan in frustration, but managed to filter out my annoyance—I hoped. "No, but I really do need to see someone quickly."

"Well..." The young woman on the phone at least pretended that she wanted to help. So far, that was much better than the other calls.

I tried for a little pity. "My symptoms have been rather alarming, and I don't think an ER visit is going to be any help."

A loud sigh puffed across the line. "Tell me what

your symptoms are, and—no promises—maybe we can fit you in on Monday or Tuesday."

That was the best offer I'd had so far.

"Rapid weight loss, persistent and unquenchable thirst, aching muscles—though that's gone now—and long periods of sleep. Oh—and I can't seem to keep food down." I reviewed my mental symptom checklist. "I think that's it."

"All right. I'll check in with the doctor, but she's quite busy today. We may not be back in touch until Monday. And if at any time you feel like there's an emergency, you should seek help from an urgent care facility or the emergency room."

"Yes, I understand that." I mentally shrugged as I gave her my contact details. Losing twenty-five pounds in days was likely a really big emergency—but I was mobile and staying hydrated. And I really, really didn't want to go to the ER. What would the ER do for me besides send me a massive bill? I was walking and talking and had no pain.

I was scrolling through alternative choices online, holding on to the ridiculous hope someone would see me before Monday, when my phone rang.

As I tapped accept, I realized it was the number for the alternative medicine clinic. "Hello?"

"This is Dr. Dobrescu. Is this Mallory Andrews?"

It hadn't even been five minutes, so the doctor obviously hadn't been *that* busy.

"Yes, that's me. Do you think you might get me in?"

"When did your symptoms start?" Brisk and businesslike, Dr. Dobrescu wasn't messing about.

"Maybe Tuesday? As I told your receptionist, I've been sleeping quite a bit, so I can't say exactly."

"Are you missing any time?"

"I'm not sure what—" I suddenly realized I had no idea how I got home from the bar. Two white wine spritzers wouldn't have that effect. "Ah, maybe."

Silence followed.

I checked to see that I hadn't accidentally ended the call, but it was still live on my end. "Dr. Dobrescu?"

"As soon as you can, come in."

"I'm sorry?"

"We'll fit you in. When can we expect you?"

The clinic had gone from "maybe Monday or Tuesday" to "come in now" in the space of minutes, and I hadn't even mentioned exactly how much weight I'd lost. I didn't think my symptoms were that specific—at least not according to Google. But given my situation, especially the part where I needed to show up at work on Monday to keep my job, I could hardly be choosy. "I can be there in forty-five minutes."

"We'll be ready for you."

I ended the call and then found myself staring at

the phone. *We'll be ready for you.* The call had been just a little bit off. Or my imagination was running wild. Probably the latter given my less-than-stellar reasoning skills on an empty stomach.

Rooting around in my closet finally produced an old tennis skirt that almost fit and an only slightly oversized T-shirt. I skipped my usual shower, because I was on a tight timeline. I felt like a narcoleptic time bomb.

As I zipped along in my flashy red Audi TT, two things bothered me. I'd never thought my car was flashy before today, and I was less comfortable driving a new sports car than I was with the sad state of my attire. I couldn't remember the last time I'd been in public looking quite so rumpled. But the normal anxiety—that "what would people think" feeling that I normally suffered—simply wasn't there. It was liberating.

The office wasn't at all what I expected; it looked like any other doctor's office. The only thing different from my regular, cranky-old-man doctor's office was the speed with which the staff ushered me into an exam room. I typically waited fifteen to thirty minutes at a minimum. And it wasn't as if the practice wasn't busy. The receptionist hadn't exaggerated. I'd parked across the street because the office's lot had been full.

I sat down on the edge of the examining table

and watched in surprise as the nurse or assistant—I wasn't sure which, because she hadn't bothered to introduce herself—disappeared out the door. She'd gone without taking a history, or commenting on when the doctor would be able to see me, or even a goodbye. Looking back, the only direct interaction I'd had with the staff was to confirm my name.

"Curiouser and curiouser." I flipped through the contacts in my phone, trying to find someone—anyone—that I could send a quick text with my location and a heads-up to check on me in an hour or so.

I didn't realize I'd spoken out loud until a woman's voice startled me with a reply. "Do you frequently feel like Alice?"

My eyes met the intent gaze of a dark-haired woman who carried a clipboard. Her delicate features and even skin tones made her age hard to determine, but I guessed anywhere between thirty and fifty. "Ah. No, actually. Just the last few days." I squinted to read her nametag: Dr. Dobrescu. "Don't you guys usually have your nurses take a history before you see patients?"

"There's some concern that you're contagious. If you don't mind, I'd like to eliminate that as a possibility before we proceed."

She still had that intent look, so I couldn't help wonder if there was a serious problem lurking. I'd stopped worrying quite so much, because—twenty-five pounds of rapid weight loss aside—I was feeling pretty good. My energy buzz hadn't faded yet. "How do you do that?"

"It's an in-house test. I just need to draw a little blood."

When I shrugged, she set her clipboard down and gloved up—twice.

"Don't you have a phlebotomist or a nurse or something for this stuff?"

"We're a small office." She approached with a metal tray.

Blatantly untrue, but I didn't think commenting would get me any answers. I watched her wrap a band around my upper arm and then swab a spot with alcohol, but after that I couldn't do it. Something about blood and needles always freaked me out—especially if it was a needle in *my* arm and *my* blood. I stared at a point on the wall, careful that I couldn't even catch what she was doing in my peripheral vision.

"You'll feel a small pinch now."

I choked on a laugh. Where did doctors learn that stuff? "Ow."

"Did that hurt?" She sounded genuinely surprised.

Really? She just shoved a needle in my arm, and she was surprised? What kind of doctor was this lady? Glancing in her direction and then quickly away when I caught sight of the tube filling with blood, I replied, "Well, it was more than a pinch."

"You said your symptoms began Tuesday?"

"I think so. That's the last time I remember being conscious."

"You can look now; I'm done."

"Also, I should mention that I've lost a lot of weight. I think maybe twenty-five pounds in the last few days. I can't be exactly sure because I hadn't weighed myself in a while, but close to that."

Still Dr. Dobrescu didn't meet my eyes. And she didn't seem surprised.

"Are you guys in touch with the CDC or something?"

Finally, I'd caught her attention. Dobrescu's head popped up from her clipboard. "What do you mean?"

She looked a little panicky.

"I just mean that you say I'm contagious, and my visit hasn't exactly been typical so far. You seem to know something about what's going on. Is there some kind of bug going around that you're on the lookout for?"

With a firm shake of her head, she said, "This will only take a moment." Finally, the woman gave me a close, intent look. Like she was peering into my soul. "Stay here."

Eyes wide, I replied as solemnly as I could, "I will."

Where the heck did she think I was going?

She wasn't gone that long, but when she came back she'd brought reinforcements. As in, a really large man who looked like he meant business. Tall, burly, and with a shaved head, I couldn't help thinking of the Mr. Clean commercials. Except Mr. Clean had a friendly, welcoming, I-want-to-clean-your-home vibe that this guy was lacking.

"Ah, is there some issue?" I scooted around on the end of the exam table, trying to decide whether to hop off—and thereby trigger some reaction from the big guy—or to stay seated and wait for Dobrescu to sic her extra-large nurse on me. "You guys never even took a history or anything. Don't you want to know about my parents' health, whether I'm taking any medications, that type of thing?"

I didn't remember being this chatty when I was nervous...but maybe the chatter would distract them, and I wouldn't get tackled.

"We just need to make sure that you're safe before you leave." Dr. Dobrescu looked down at her clipboard. "How long ago did you first fall ill?"

The big guy blocked the door. And now that I looked past the shaved head, I noticed he wasn't wearing clogs—unlike the rest of the staff—and he wasn't wearing nurse scrubs. Hm. Not a nurse.

"Last Tuesday I was fine. I told you that before. So—what?—that was six days ago. You're a little bit freaking me out right now." And, of course, a little meant a lot. I glanced at the big guy.

She shared a look with the man then made a note. "Have you felt any violent urges?"

"Noooo."

Dr. Dobrescu looked up at me like she didn't buy it.

"You're making me very uncomfortable, and I'm considering my exit strategies. I'm all about the flight and not the fight."

Dr. Dobrescu scribbled furiously.

"Ah—you don't mean violence to myself, do you?"

The doctor's head bobbed up. "Have you been feeling a desire to self-harm? Or any suicidal thoughts?"

The woman looked much too excited about the prospect. I was starting to feel like a lab experiment.

"Not even a little. Are you going to tell me what's going on?"

She reached into her lab coat and pulled something out. She thrust it at me, and I grabbed it without thinking.

In my right hand, I held a tube filled with dark red...blood? "Ack!"

The vial fell from my fingers. It bounced off the

edge of the exam table and then shattered on the floor. Bits of glass scattered, and blood seeped around the shards. "Nuts." I turned to the doctor with a nasty look. "Why would you do that? Couldn't you tell how much having my blood drawn freaked me out?"

The doctor had retreated to stand next to Mr. Clean near the door as I'd spoken.

Before I could worry much about the frantic scribbling and hushed whispers, my stomach rebelled. It started with a gentle roiling sensation when the odor of the blood first hit me. But then the smell filled my nose, overpowering the doctor's perfume, the disinfectant odor in the room; every other scent faded under the stench of blood.

And I puked.

Once my stomach had voided the small amount of liquid it held—I'd chugged bottled water on the drive over—I dry-heaved for a while.

With nose pinched and hand covering my mouth, I pointed at the blood without looking at it. "Hey, could you get rid of it? Please?" I swallowed, trying not to heave again.

I hadn't realized that during all of my heaving the big guy had left. But thankfully he returned now with a mop bucket that exuded a strong chemical odor and began mopping up the mess. He didn't look very happy about it.

"Why would you do that?" I asked the doctor with my hand still over my nose and mouth.

I swallowed and tried not to gag again. The odor was muted but it was still there. I leaned to my left, trying to see past Mr. Clean as he wielded the mop.

"The blood?" she asked. "It's part of the test."

I gave her an exasperated look. "You didn't get how squeamish I am when you drew my blood? You really needed to test that?"

Although that wasn't entirely true. Usually it was my own blood that made me cringe. And, weirdly, I *knew* that blood hadn't been mine. I didn't linger on *how* exactly I knew that.

She looked as annoyed with me as I felt, and she practically snapped, "Vampires aren't afraid of blood."

I considered whether I'd heard her correctly, decided I hadn't, and then decided I had. And that was it. I doubled over, and I laughed till I cried.

I laughed so hard that my side started to cramp up—and I kept laughing.

Several minutes later, my hand firmly clutching my aching side, I looked up to find Dr. Dobrescu standing alone near the door. Again, the big guy had managed to leave without me noticing—and this time with a huge yellow janitor's bucket on wheels. He was a sneaky one.

"You're a vampire." She said as if by making the

statement sound factual, it was somehow less ridiculous.

"No. I'm not. You're certifiable."

She clutched that darn clipboard close to her body, like a shield. Against me. The vampire. "You are."

"I'm not. And I'm not going to play that game. Vampires aren't real. And clearly you're not a real doctor. Did you even go to medical school?"

Dr. Dobrescu named a prestigious medical school on the West Coast.

"Oh." I looked around the very normal office, with its normal exam table and normal posters. There were even those little canisters with cotton balls in them. "Well, maybe you're a doctor, but that doesn't mean you're not crazy."

She sighed. "How did you lose twenty-five pounds in a handful of days?"

"Starvation and a crazy-fast metabolism." Obviously. Never mind that the same question had been burbling around in my head since I woke from my comatose state.

She raised her eyebrows.

"What? That could happen." That so could *not* happen. "When's Mr. Clean coming back? Because I will not go quietly if you try to commit me. Or—" I made a stabbing motion. "You know, stake me."

Dr. Dobrescu's eyes grew large in her face. I

thought I'd finally managed to shock her. Because me being a vampire hadn't done it. A vampire. Come on.

"Anton has determined that you're not currently a safety risk."

"*I'm* not a safety risk? What about you? With your blood vials and your weird bedside manner, not to mention your delusions."

Dr. Dobrescu stepped further into the room, gave me a speculative look, then came to some conclusion —because her attitude changed. She looked less businesslike. A little droopy, even. She sat down on the little rolling chair that all exam rooms seem to come equipped with and rolled closer to the table.

She assumed a solemn expression. "I am very sorry to have to tell you this, but you're no longer human. A virus has invaded your body, resulting in certain...changes."

Virus—that was a word I could grab hold of. Chew on a little. A scary word—but not a crazy one. The rest... My brain did a little la-la-la to the rest of what she was saying. "So what's the prognosis?"

I skipped over the fact that I was asking for medical information from a woman who had clearly lost her marbles.

"Unknown. The disease will most likely progress quite rapidly, but the end result is...uncertain. It's my understanding that vampires require blood to complete the transformation."

"I'm sorry, did you say transformation?" I narrowed my eyes. "And what do you mean 'uncertain'?" I looked around the room. I was in a doctor's office and a doctor was telling me I might croak from a disease that didn't exist. Couldn't exist. Because when a doctor says the prognosis is uncertain—that has to include the big "D." Dead. Then I remembered: crazy lady talking. I swallowed a groan. Transformation meant transformation into an undead vampire. "Are we talking about me ceasing to breathe, turning into a bat, and being afraid of garlic and crosses?"

Now she was looking at me like *I* was the crazy one.

I gritted my teeth and tried again. "When you say transformation, do you mean I will join the ranks of the undead?"

Good grief. If ever there was a phrase I never would have thought would pass my lips, that one scored in the top ten.

"Possibly. But there's also the very real possibility of regular dead. Not undead dead, just dead dead." Then she winced. "Your life in any form might end."

"Because I'm not into sucking blood? You have got to be kidding me. And, by the way, I feel fine. So how can you know what exactly this virus is doing to me?"

Mumbo jumbo doctor stuff followed, but the best I could understand, my body was supposedly going through some sort of transformation—the improved appearance of my skin, as well as other as yet undiscovered "perks"—and that this transformation was supposed to be fueled in part by the consumption of large quantities of blood.

"Hold on. I'm not"—my gag reflex kicked in, and I swallowed—"drinking blood. That is beyond disgusting."

"That's just it—if you can't consume blood, you'll starve. I suspect that had something to do with your rapid weight loss."

"Can't you just inject me? Give me a transfusion?"

"I don't think so. Humans can't digest blood, and vamps have to digest it to obtain—whatever they need from it. I'm a human doctor, and not an expert on vampirism. I'm only aware of the condition because of an incident with a client a few weeks ago. Anton was assigned to handle the resulting situation." Dr. Dobrescu crossed her arms.

And for only the second time since I'd stepped into the office, I noticed her. Not her lab coat or clipboard, but her. Fair-skinned with dark hair and light eyes. She didn't *look* like a crazy person.

"So, I'll suck it up and drink some blood." I choked back the hysterical giggle on the tip of my tongue. Who knew I'd get all punny when confronted with my own mortality?

"I don't think it's going to be that simple, but I hope it is. I hope I'm wrong. Again, I'm no expert—I only know what I've been told recently—and how to test for the virus."

"And who to contact if there's a safety risk." That phrase had an ominous ring to it. Then it hit me that I was inches from being designated one. "What would Anton have done if I had been a safety risk?"

The doc looked uncomfortable. Great—that couldn't be good.

"Well, is there at least a how-to manual? Do I get a mentor? A consultant? Anything?" I scrubbed my face with both hands, then peeked between them to look at the doctor. Her green eyes looked kindly back. "I've drunk the Kool-Aid."

She reached into her lab coat pocket and pulled out a business card. "Anton is a member of the Society. They're your best resource for information on the virus and what to expect. Until I have more time...I just don't know very much. And since I'm not one of you, the Society isn't making what information they have available to me." Once I'd taken the card, she tilted her head. "Ah, he did say if you feel a murderous rage coming on, call the number on the back."

I accepted the card. "A murderous rage?"

Looking down, I found that she'd handed me a thick cream card, reminiscent of the old-style calling cards. It read simply: Anton. And underneath was a local number. I flipped it over to find a hastily scrawled number following the letters ER. Emergency room? Emergency? Ernest Riddle? Elijah Rockford? Some other random guy's name with the initials ER?

With a sinking feeling, I realized I'd bought in completely. The freakish smell of the blood, my reaction to it, my bizarre symptoms...it all meant something. And I *was* different. On some fundamental level, I had changed. Like a knot inside me had loosened.

"They don't expect me to last past a few days, do they?" I asked.

"I honestly don't know."

But I did. Because if this was all real, if I really was on the cusp of vampirism, then I had to be a huge security risk. I could blab to anyone. Or could I? Because who would believe me? I scrubbed my face again.

"Any last words of advice, doc?"

"Since it seems you can hold down water, that's a good place to start. And I guess experiment with what you can tolerate." She rolled her chair away and stood up. "And call the number. I truly hope they can help you."

As we walked down the hall together, she stopped suddenly. "I can't believe that I almost forgot. Your condition has to be kept secret. There are consequences for sharing the information broadly. Or with your family. Or your friends. It's best to just keep it to yourself."

"Yep—I figured that."

Dr. Dobrescu was about to walk me out the door of her clinic without taking any payment—or answering the tens of questions I suddenly realized I hadn't asked. The most pressing one popped out as we approached the exit. "How did I catch this virus?"

She raised her eyebrows, surprised by the question. "You were bitten."

Dr. Dobrescu pushed me out the door then shut it firmly, me on one side and her on the other.

Join Mallory on her journey of vampiric discovery.
Download your copy of
***Adventures of a Vegan Vamp* now!**

ABOUT THE AUTHOR

When Cate's not tapping away at her keyboard or in deep contemplation of her next fanciful writing project, she's sweeping up hairy dust bunnies and watching British mysteries.

Cate is from Austin, Texas (where many of her stories take place) but has recently migrated north to Boise, Idaho, where soup season (her favorite time of year) lasts more than two weeks.

She's worked as an attorney, a dog trainer, and in various other positions, but writer is the hands-down winner. She's thankful readers keep reading, so she can keep writing!

For bonus materials and updates, visit her website to join her mailing list: www.CateLawley.com.

CPSIA information can be obtained
at www.ICGtesting.com
Printed in the USA
BVHW042100180121
598113BV00021B/343